D1743657

WITHDRAWN

CUMBRIA COUNTY LIBRARY

The Strongest Man in the World

A tragicomedy in three acts
by

BARRY COLLINS

FABER AND FABER
London   Boston

First published in Great Britain in 1980
by Faber and Faber Limited
3 Queen Square London WC1N 3AU
Typeset by An Grianán
Printed in Great Britain by
Lowe & Brydone Printers Limited Thetford
All rights reserved

© *Barry Collins 1980*

British Library Cataloguing in Publication Data

Collins, Barry
The strongest man in the world.
I. Title
822'.9'14   PR6053.04248S/

ISBN 0-571-11111-4

CHARACTERS

IVAN D SHUKHOV a young miner
NATASHA his fiancée
MOTHER SHUKHOV
ALEXEI ⎫
NIKOLAI ⎪
BORIS ⎪
LOPAKHIN ⎬ miners
DIMITROV ⎪
BRODSKY ⎭
DIMITROVNA ⎫ miners' wives
MRS BRODSKY ⎭
BASIL SEMYONOV a journalist
A. PRISIPKIN an official in the Soviet Ministry of Sport
PROF ABULADZE an expert in proletarian anatomy
GENERAL IMMANUEL VELIKOVSKY (retired)
SUPERINTENDENT
SHAGRADOV his deputy
MAJOR KALOGRADOV an Olympic weightlifting coach
DIAGHILEV a masseur
DR ANDREYEV
DOBROVOLSKY a weightlifter
ANDREI ⎫ television technicians
SASHA ⎭
1st OFFICIAL
2nd OFFICIAL
3rd OFFICIAL
4th OFFICIAL
THE CARETAKER OF THE HALL OF HEROES
1st JUDGE
2nd JUDGE
3rd JUDGE
PROSECUTOR
PROTOPOPOV a court guard
DR VERA LYUBOVNA
ASYLUM DIRECTOR
VANITSIN his deputy
A NURSE

LEONID a ward orderly
DIMSHITS a hut warder
PETROV
KOTELIANSKY
TARASCHENKO
GAVRILOV   } Asylum 'politicals'
KOVALCHUK
PETLIURA

NOTE

Running time (with two intervals): three hours.

With careful doubling, the play may be performed by twelve actors
—eight men and four women. Five players would retain their single
parts throughout: IVAN, NATASHA, MOTHER SHUKHOV,
SEMYONOV and VERA. The other seven would share the more
important remaining characters—miners playing bureaucrats, playing
policemen, doctors, spies, prisoners, etc. Parts lost would include:
the MINERS' WIVES, DIMITROVNA and MRS BRODSKY; the
GYMNASTS; the VILLAGERS; the ASYLUM GUARDS.

The necessary textual changes are as follows:

Pages 11, 12: only two miners are rescued.

Page 12: speeches of DIMITROVNA and MRS BRODSKY are
taken by MOTHER SHUKHOV.

Page 23: PRISIPKIN makes his platform speeches to the audience.

Act 1, Scenes 5, 6: KALOGRADOV does the lifting demonstrations
himself and helps the doctor and masseur apply the irons and
beam.

Page 54: FOURTH OFFICIAL will be a man.

Act 3, Scene 1: no female JUDGE.

Page 78: KOVALCHUK is played by a woman.

Page 83: DIMSHITS makes the arrests, armed with a machine-gun,
and thus needs extra lines:
DIMSHITS: What the blazes—?...Shukhov! Oh, sweet fuckin'
Christ!... [*To VERA*] They've done it to spite me!
VERA: Arrest them.

The Strongest Man in the World was first performed at the Nottingham Playhouse on 18 October 1978. The cast was as follows:

IVAN D SHUKHOV	Nick Stringer
NATASHA	Tina Marian
MOTHER SHUKHOV	Margot Thomas
ALEXEI	Colin Bruce
NIKOLAI	Walter Macmonagle
BORIS	Sean Baker
LOPAKHIN	Nick Dunning
DIMITROV	Hywel David
BRODSKY	John Flint
DIMITROVNA	Angela Phillips
MRS BRODSKY	Frankie Cosgrave
BASIL SEMYONOV	Ian Jentle
A. PRISIPKIN	Christopher Ettridge
PROF ABULADZE	Tim Meats
GENERAL IMMANUEL VELIKOVSKY	Ron Flanagan
SUPERINTENDENT	Nick Hughes
SHAGRADOV	Roger Simcox
MAJOR KALOGRADOV	Garfield Morgan
DIAGHILEV	Michael Mears
DR ANDREYEV	Tom Wilkinson
DOBROVOLSKY	John Flint
ANDREI	Hywel David
SASHA	Nick Dunning
1st OFFICIAL	Michael Mears
2nd OFFICIAL	Tim Meats
3rd OFFICIAL	Walter Macmonagle
4th OFFICIAL	Angela Phillips
CARETAKER	Frankie Cosgrave
1st JUDGE	Hywel David
2nd JUDGE	Roger Simcox
3rd JUDGE	Colin Bruce
PROSECUTOR	Tim Meats
PROTOPOPOV	John Flint

DR VERA LYUBOVNA	Frankie Cosgrave
ASYLUM DIRECTOR	Walter Macmonagle
VANITSIN	Nick Hughes
A NURSE	Angela Phillips
LEONID	Nick Dunning
DIMSHITS	Ron Flanagan
PETROV	Sean Baker
KOTELIANSKY	Hywel David
TARASCHENKO	John Flint
GAVRILOV	Garfield Morgan
KOVALCHUK	Michael Mears
PETLIURA	Colin Bruce

Directed by Geoffrey Reeves and John Russell-Brown
Designed by David Collis

ACT ONE

SCENE ONE

Stage in darkness. At rear, a large screen is illuminated: upon it, a huge red flag, bearing the hammer and sickle and the legend 'Union of Soviet Socialist Republics'. Briefly, the blaring sound of the Soviet national anthem. Screen picture changes to a pithead scene, with winding gear, etc, in the heart of a plain, with mountains in the background. Stage right, slowly rising, the dim, eerie light of underground pit workings: timbers can be seen at some kind of road crossing point.
Enter, four MINERS, helmeted, dirty, naked to the waist. NIKOLAI, the eldest, white-haired, is in his fifties; ALEXEI and BORIS are nearing middle-age; the other, IVAN, is younger—about twenty-two, thickset, perhaps deep-chested, firmly-muscled, but no Hercules.... The three older men sit, stir about for boxes, prepare provisions, etc; the younger man stays at some distance, standing.

ALEXEI: [*Singing, as they leave the tunnel*]
        The supervisor's in disgrace,
        He spends his moonlights down the face:
NIKOLAI: [*Taking up the song*]
        While Ivan Shukhov blows him kisses—
BORIS: [*With the raucous finale*]
        And fucks the sweet arse off his missus!
    [*Loud laughter. IVAN, ignoring them, seems preoccupied.*]
ALEXEI: What's she like, then, Vanya?
BORIS: Drops you a quid or two, does she?
ALEXEI: Better watch it, lad: on't seam all day, on't nest all night.
NIKOLAI: Bloody stallion!
BORIS: [*To NIKOLAI*] Old goat!
    [*A creaking noise is heard from inside the mine workings.*]
IVAN: Listen! [*Pause*]
ALEXEI: It's the boss's bed creaking.
BORIS: No chance—Vanya's bust it...haven't you, Vanya?
IVAN: Ballocks!
ALEXEI: Don't be shy.
BORIS: Mishkina's not shy: she's selling tickets.... Twice nightly!
ALEXEI: Whadda performance!

BORIS: Like a young bull, she says.

NIKOLAI: [*Glumly*] Bull! Who needs a bull to break a bed, these days? If yer cat farts, yer bed shudders.

BORIS: You shouldn't sleep with your cat. [*They laugh.*]

ALEXEI: What did she tell him, Vanya?

IVAN: Tell who?

BORIS: Mishkin, stupid!

ALEXEI: About the bed....

IVAN: [*Grinning*] Said she fell off the ladder, dustin' Comrade Lenin's portrait.

BORIS: Lenin's portrait!

ALEXEI: In Mishkin's bedroom?

BORIS: [*Fiercely*] Bureaucrat!

IVAN: She hangs her stockings on it.

ALEXEI: [*Eating*] Where does she hang her petticoat?

IVAN: On the ikon.

BORIS: No wonder the bed broke!

ALEXEI: Under all that sin.

NIKOLAI: [*Ironic, lugubrious*] Sin—now there's a thing. For yer average sin, give me a bourgeois bed every time.... Mine wer' a fourposter, wi' curtains an' swansdown pillers, a two-foot mattress—an' a porcelain pisspot.

BORIS: Not your Chinese porcelain pisspot?

NIKOLAI: [*Deadpan*] Aye, fer containin' the yeller peril.... [*More laughter. IVAN is still fretting.*]

IVAN: Listen! I heard it again!

ALEXEI: Stop blatherin'! You give me the creeps.

BORIS: S'more ner he gives Natasha—poor love, keepin' her little treasure warm, all by 'erself...in 'er little bottom drawer.

ALEXEI: Dun't want a ring through his nose, do you, Vanya?

NIKOLAI: [*Wagging a finger*] Bugger't ring, lad: you look for't right bed. Tell't times, you can, by't state o't blasted beds.

BORIS: Here we go again.

ALEXEI: Me and my fourposter!

NIKOLAI: [*Innocent*] Well, got it from a prince, didn't I? 1917 —durin' the revolution... Prince Bolkonsky! Chopped it up for firewood in 1918.

IVAN: [*The sucker*] You weren't even born in 1918!

NIKOLAI: No, I wer' born in 1920, an' they 'aven't made a decent bed since.

BORIS: Is that so? What about yer thirties model—six feet deep, lasts for ever. [*IVAN turns away, towards the mouth of the tunnel. BORIS follows, taunting.*] Ivan believes in the solidarity of the revolutionary working-class bed!

ALEXEI: [*Mocking*] 'Cept his feet stick out o' the end.

NIKOLAI: [*Cackling*] Need summat to shove on, don't you.

10

Vanya? [*For a lark, ALEXEI and BORIS grab IVAN and lift him, so his feet are kicking thin air.*]

IVAN: Gerroff!

ALEXEI: Comrades, when the feet don't fit the bed, do you chop off the feet or change the bed?

BORIS: You curl up an' bloody die!

IVAN: [*Angry, as they let him fall*] Before the revolution, our sort never had beds.

ALEXEI, BORIS, NIKOLAI: [*Singing sarcastically*]
The Internationale unites the human race...

IVAN: [*Yelling at them*] Listen, damn you, listen!

BORIS: Woodworm! S'woodworm. Ever thought of it? Mile of earth up top: say, ten worms a square yard—that's a helluva lot o' worms, give or take a ton o' Jew's harps.

IVAN: It's the roof!

ALEXEI: Course it's the flamin' roof.

IVAN: On the low seam...Dimitrov's down there!

ALEXEI: Look, Dimitrov's been down there for years. Loves that low seam, Dimitrov. Talks to him, see, timber an' all. He'll not quit till she cracks—an' she'll not crack till Christmas.
[*Again, the creaking noise, nearer, and much louder.*]

IVAN: It's going! I told you! It's going!

ALEXEI: Dimitrov said—

BORIS: Shag Dimitrov! Let's scarper!

IVAN: We can't leave them.

NIKOLAI: No choice, lad.

IVAN: Maybe I can hold this beam.... Call them out.

BORIS: He's crackers, he's bloody crackers!
[*Before anyone can stop him, IVAN has entered the tunnel and, facing the audience, has planted himself beneath the falling beam, holding it up with arms and shoulders.*]

NIKOLAI, ALEXEI: [*On their knees*] Dimitrov! The roof! Dimitrov! [*From further away, the crash of a tunnel collapsing.*]

ALEXEI: Too late!

BORIS: They're a quarter mile down!

IVAN: Call again!

NIKOLAI: [*Desperately*] Dimitrov, get up here—get up here, can't you? [*More noise. Slowly, IVAN is being buckled.*]

ALEXEI: [*Trying to yank him away*] Vanya! Tunnel's crumbling!

IVAN: [*Face contorted*] Let go!

BORIS: You'll have us all killed!

ALEXEI: [*On his knees*] Dimitrov!

NIKOLAI: They're coming.... Hang on, Vanya!
[*NIKOLAI drags two MINERS out of the tunnel around IVAN's legs. BORIS and ALEXEI are helping IVAN keep up the beam.*]

11

IVAN: How many more?
DIMITROV: [*Yelling*] Lopakhin, Brodsky—faster! Faster!
   [*Another miner, LOPAKHIN, is dragged from the tunnel, coughing badly. IVAN is now on his knees in great pain.*]
NIKOLAI: Ring the alarm!
   [*Boris rushes across stage right, to press an alarm buzzer. Gradually the sound fills the theatre.*]
ALEXEI: [*Yelling, almost beside himself*] Brodsky!
DIMITROV: He's too weak.
NIKOLAI: Brodsky—you old sod!
IVAN: It's slipping! Save yourselves!
ALEXEI: [*Trying to pull him free*] Vanya!
IVAN: I can't.
ALEXEI: Vanya!
IVAN: Run! Run! [*The untrapped MINERS scramble and are dragged off-stage, right.*]
IVAN: [*A long, echoing howl*] Brodsky!
   [*Immediately, a thundering noise, sounds of collapse. Blackout. Cut alarm.*]

SCENE TWO

Lights rise again, stage left, providing a dusky area. On-screen, close-up, silhouetted, pithead winding gear. At front-stage, left, a group of women, scarved and shawled, waiting. Slightly apart, sitting, cross-legged, on the ground, is MOTHER SHUKHOV —sewing. Beside her, anxiously stands NATASHA. The girl is sturdy, dark, pretty—about twenty: the MOTHER has the seamed, patient face of suffering and poverty.

NATASHA: How long is it now?
MOTHER SHUKHOV: Six hours.
NATASHA: How much longer?
MOTHER SHUKHOV: Took three days to find his father.
NATASHA: [*Emotionally*] Will they get him out, Mother Shukhov?
MOTHER SHUKHOV: They usually do, lass, one way or t'other.
   [*She carries on sewing. NATASHA turns aside to the other women, weeping.*]
DIMITROVNA: Cryin' won't help.... Cryin' comes later.
NATASHA: How can she sit there like that?
MRS BRODSKY: Collier's wench, aren't you? Tha mun get used to waitin'.
DIMITROVNA: While they were seekin' old man Shukhov, she embroidered a whole tablecloth. When they fetched him out,

12

wi' the blanket over his face, she just kept on sewing.... I
bought that cloth from her—after: it had little round stains
in one corner that'd never wash clean.

[*At stage right, spotlight suddenly on the collapsed pit workings. Helmeted MINERS are seen crawling through the debris,
calling.*]

BORIS: Shukhov!

ALEXEI: Vanya Shukhov!

DIMITROV: Brodsky!

[*No reply. The search goes on—the debris is lifted away and
cleared off-stage. Cut spotlight. At stage left, NATASHA
returns to MOTHER SHUKHOV, kneeling beside her as she
sews.*]

MOTHER SHUKHOV: Something had to happen today...three
black crows on the fence all mornin'—never moved, all
mornin'. T'were the same the day his father died—and his
brother—three black crows....

NATASHA: Why didn't you shoo them away? [*MOTHER
SHUKHOV looks up at NATASHA for the first time. Spotlight again at stage right; the searching MINERS call—and
clear the debris.*]

ALEXEI: Vanya, can you hear me?

BORIS: Yell out, Shukhov!

DIMITROV: Brodsky! Brodsky—where are you? [*Spotlight off.*]

NATASHA: What are you sewing?

MOTHER SHUKHOV: Sheets. Could be for cradles, could be
for coffins.

[*NATASHA stifles a cry.... Stage right, spotlight: the
MINERS find IVAN and BRODSKY.*]

ALEXEI: There! Under the beam!

BORIS: Is he alive?

ALEXEI: I'll say...heart like a bellows.

DIMITROV: What about Brodsky?

ALEXEI: Vanya's on top of him.... They'll need stretchers.

[*Spotlight off. Enter NIKOLAI, rushing to the WOMEN, waiting, at left.*]

NIKOLAI: Supervisor Mishkin asks me to tell you that miners .
Brodsky and Shukhov are safe!

NATASHA: Mother Shukhov—he's alive! He's alive!

MOTHER SHUKHOV: [*Still sewing*] Aye, but is he hurt?

[*Exit NIKOLAI. Spotlight on, stage right.*]

ALEXEI: Vanya, we've come back for you lad.

[*IVAN and BRODSKY are put on stretchers.*]

BORIS: Easy does it. [*By now, the debris of the collapse is cleared.
Light at left is raised: stage now fully lit. NATASHA and the
waiting WOMEN rush forward, excitedly.*]

13

NATASHA: Vanya! Oh, Vanya!
    [*Enter NIKOLAI, rushing across to MOTHER SHUKHOV.*]
NIKOLAI: Not a mark on him! Just a clatter in his ears. S'a
    miracle, widow-woman—a miracle!
MOTHER SHUKHOV: Vanya doesn't believe in miracles.
    [*NIKOLAI, MINERS, STRETCHER-VICTIMS and WOMEN
    exit. MOTHER SHUKHOV gathers up her sewing.
    NATASHA has waited for her.*]
NATASHA: What about your black crows now, Mother
    Shukhov?
MOTHER SHUKHOV: Ah, lass, I put 'em some bread down
    round about noon-day an' they come an' took it an' flew off
    to somebody else's fence. [*She gives the sheet to NATASHA.*]
    Sheet'll save for a crib, then.
NATASHA: [*Bitter, despite herself*] Give it his fancy woman.
MOTHER SHUKHOV: [*Smiling*] Don't be daft, lass. Men're
    better for knowin' what they're doin'. Vanya's young: great
    body on him—thinks it'll last for ever: they all do.... You
    get him wed—get some bairns off him...'fore them crows
    come callin' back. [*MOTHER SHUKHOV and NATASHA
    exit. Blackout.*]

SCENE THREE

*On-screen, a full-length photograph of IVAN SHUKHOV, naked.
Lights up—revealing a large desk, with three seats, three telephones.
Also a telex machine. Enter, excitedly, in line abreast, the COM-
MITTEE—a small, bald, bull-necked general, a rather sinister-
looking senior Party bureaucrat and a tall, lean, bespectacled
professor. All three gaze admiringly at the screen.*
PRISIPKIN: Beautiful, isn't he?
VELIKOVSKY: Magnificent!
ABULADZE: Thoroughbred proletarian.
VELIKOVSKY: And a hero to boot.
PRISIPKIN: [*With a flowing gesture*] Comrades, let me introduce
    to you, Soviet Man, in all his majesty: candidate 6347/2,
    Shukhov, Ivan Denisovich.... And comrades, at this eleventh
    hour, at this moment of crisis in our personal fortunes, let us
    admit [*Whispering*] we have our friend Semyonov to thank
    for finding him. [*Enter, stage left, BASIL SEMYONOV,
    journalist, smoking a cigar and pushing his own, smaller desk,
    complete with telephone and old-fashioned typewriter, which
    he sets at downstage corner. He addresses the audience.*]
SEMYONOV: Semyonov! That's me. Basil Nicolayevich Semyo-

nov: human affairs correspondent of the Government newspaper, *Truth*, or, as it is affectionately known in the trade, *Fiction*.... And these three gentlemen, permit me, comprise the emergency committee to discover the strongest man in the world, codename: 'Mr Big'.... From left to right, General Immanuel Velikovsky, war hero, retired; Comrade Alexander Prisipkin, First Deputy Minister of Sport, and Doctor Leonid Abuladze, Professor of Anatomy, Moscow Academy of Science. [*At their introduction, they turn to greet SEMYONOV, in relieved mood.*]

PRISIPKIN: Ah, Semyonov, my dear chap, it seems our search is over. How can we thank you enough?

SEMYONOV: Well, there is the matter of the—

PRISIPKIN: Later, dear fellow, later: we can all expect our little... emoluments.

SEMYONOV: [*Aside*] Emoluments! Top-floor flat overlooking the Volga Canal, holidays in Astrakhan, the blonde on the fur counter at the State grocery store.... Emoluments, he says. They get the emoluments, I don't even get the groceries. What did I expect—promotion? [*As SEMYONOV speaks, the COMMITTEE establishes itself around the desk and PRISIPKIN, the chairman, produces and duly bangs a gavel.*]

PRISIPKIN: To business, comrades, to business.... First, I think a little reminder of the enormity of our task...Victor, if you please, the President! [*PRISIPKIN calls out, as if to some operator at the rear of the theatre. The COMMITTEE stands. A slow, deep voice rings, biblically, through the auditorium.*]

VOICE OF PRESIDENT: Comrades, we approach a critical stage in the struggle for the human mind! [*The COMMITTEE applauds vigorously—matching the tumultuous applause on the tape.*]

PRISIPKIN: Thank you, Victor.

VOICE OF PRESIDENT: July 1980! At last, Moscow will stage the Olympic Games. [*Again the COMMITTEE applauds —matching the tape applause.*]

PRISIPKIN: [*More touchily*] Thank you, Victor.

VOICE OF PRESIDENT: On the battlefield of sport, Mother Russia will unveil the New Man. [*Applause on tape.*]

PRISIPKIN: [*Yelling*] I said thank you, Victor!

VOICE OF PRESIDENT: Yes, the New Man: born of the revolution, tempered in the eternal flame— [*At last the tape is cut.*]

PRISIPKIN: [*Returning to his seat*] In other words, comrades, the Olympic Maxi-Weightlifting Champion...as if we could pull him out of a hat or accelerate a Five-Year Plan! [*PRISIPKIN pulls himself up short—what has he said? With a frightened laugh...*] Just my little joke...

ABULADZE: [*Nervously*] Ha, ha. The chairman will have his
    little joke... [*There is a moment's frozen silence, as the
    COMMITTEE look at each other, then over their shoulders
    and around the stage. Suddenly, VELIKOVSKY passes a
    note to his colleagues, and, in basso profondo, bursts into
    song—'Kalinka'—waving his arms to encourage the others. At
    a signal from VELIKOVSKY, all three use the chorus as cover
    for a manic search for bugging equipment. SEMYONOV
    watches disdainfully. PRISIPKIN finds the bug in one of the
    telephones. He removes it, screams into it and then hammers
    it to death on the desk. The COMMITTEE resume their seats.*]
PRISIPKIN: Frankly, Semyonov, we were beginning to despair—last
    week's applicant sliced off a nipple in the chest expanders. I
    left it at the Ministry with a chitty for compensation, but it
    got lost in the filing system.... I tell you, this chap, er, Shukhov,
    is the answer to our prayers.
SEMYONOV: [*Writing in his notebook*] 'The answer to our
    prayers!'
PRISIPKIN: No, no! You're not quoting me, are you? Prayers? A
    figure of speech. There was no doubt—it was...inevitable—just
    a matter of time.
SEMYONOV: July 23rd, to be precise.... I was sent to investigate
    a heroic mine rescue at the village of Sheremestvo, south of
    Krasnodar...
ABULADZE: [*Interrupting*] Is it true he propped up a roof-fall
    single-handed?
VELIKOVSKY: On his shoulders?
SEMYONOV: Quite true.
VELIKOVSKY: [*Amazed*] The Russian Atlas!
PRISIPKIN: [*Crushingly*] Atlas, my dear General, bore up the sky:
    candidate Shukhov held up the earth: neither exploit qualifies
    for the Olympic Games. To win a gold medal, Shukhov must
    lift weights. More prosaic, I agree. The problem before us is
    whether we can make him lift bigger weights than anyone else.
    [*The COMMITTEE turn to the screen.*] Professor...?
ABULADZE: Oh, unquestionably! Victor! [*He approaches the
    screen with a pointing stick.*] Note the massive development
    of the sternum—
VELIKOVSKY: Pardon?
ABULADZE: The chest.... As you will see, the shoulders—back
    —thighs—even calves—are also of remarkable quality.
    [*Matching the lecture, the screen-picture changes, showing the
    relevant parts of IVAN's anatomy.*] Altogether, I detect only
    a single flaw: the forearms—they appear to be marked—there
    appear to be tattoos. I am not happy about the, er, tattoos.
PRISIPKIN: Victor—close-up, please, right forearm. [*On-screen*

comes an enlargement of IVAN's penis. Enraged...] No,
Victor! ...how many more times? [*The right forearm is shown
instead. It carries the words: 'I love U'.*] Thank you, Victor.

VELIKOVSKY: [*Scornful*] 'I love U'?

PRISIPKIN: Victor, the other arm. [*Close-up of the left forearm.*]
'I love U'. What does it mean?

VELIKOVSKY: It's a wench he loves.... [*Bawdy laugh.*]

PRISIPKIN: [*Annoyed*] Out of the question.

ABULADZE: [*Academically*] I'm not aware of any scientific
objection to the mating instinct.

PRISIPKIN: I object to the tattoos.

SEMYONOV: It's only a joke.

PRISIPKIN: The Olympic Games are not a joke.

ABULADZE: To remove them would leave scars—most unsightly.

PRISIPKIN: Very well: they must be altered—to 'I love the USSR'.
[*Tattoo picture disappears.*] How touching! The alphabet of
patriotism! Let us hope it is borne out by the secret service
report. [*An electronic bleep. The telex is heard—ticking.*]
Extraordinary! [*Another bleep: more ticking: paper spews
out of the machine.*] General, would you oblige?

VELIKOVSKY: [*Blustering*] Damned if I will! I'm not your
messenger boy, sir.

PRISIPKIN: [*With icy control*] May I remind you, General—I am
the senior member of this committee. And may I advise you
that yesterday I received a communication from the President
himself, in the following terms: 'Prisipkin, if you haven't
found that weightlifter within the week, I'll have your balls
—battered! And that goes for Abuladze and Velikovsky!'
[*VELIKOVSKY returns to the desk, swathed in paper, which
he dumps on PRISIPKIN.*]

PRISIPKIN: Excellent, General.... Now then, the police report...
[*Reading*] 'Subject an exemplary Russian. Good Party Member'—you see!... [*Now, hurrying through.*] School—ideolog-
ically sound...Soviet Youth Movement.... Three times topped
the individual coal quota for his district. Age, twenty-three.
Height: one metre 80; weight: 90 kilograms; health: good....
Semyonov, can you add to this summary?

SEMYONOV: [*Checking from his notebook*] Yes. The family
have lived in Sheremstvo for generations. His grandfather
sailed on the Potemkin and gave his life for the revolution;
his father and brother were killed in the mine, an aunt and
three uncles died defending Volgograd against the fascists.

ABULADZE: [*Dreadful thought*] I take it Shukhov survived the
accident?

SEMYONOV: Oh yes, he's recovering in the local hospital.

VELIKOVSKY: [*Sarcastic*] Has he ever done any weightlifting?

SEMYONOV: No.

PRISIPKIN: A detail—at this stage, a mere detail. I shall place an
immediate call. [*PRISIPKIN picks up his telephone.*]
Hello. Get me Sheremestvo hospital.... [*Turning to his col-
leagues.*] While we're waiting, we are agreed that Shukhov is
our Mr Big? [*All three hands go up.*] Victor, full portrait!
[*The nude picture reappears, from another angle. Grandi-
loquently...*] The New Man! Ah, hello, is that the hospital at
Sheremestvo? Speak up, please. Give me the superintendent...
What do you mean, 'He's in bed'? [*To the COMMITTEE*]
They're all in bed! I know it's the middle of the night! Look
here, who are you? Very well, never mind. True servants of
the State never sleep! Listen: I am speaking from Moscow
with the direct authority of the Supreme Soviet. My name is
A.L. Prisipkin, First Deputy Minister of Sport...Sport!.... Yes
—the miner. No expense is to be spared in his treatment,
understand? The patient Shukhov is to be given everything
he wishes everything! [*He slams down the phone.*] There,
gentlemen—a few hours' sleep and we leave for Sheremestvo,
to call candidate Shukhov to his destiny.

VELIKOVSKY: Sheremestvo's fifteen hundred kilometres away!

ABULADZE: Near the Caucasus. It'll take two days.

PRISIPKIN: For Russia, no sacrifice is too great—even the prov-
incial railway service...Semyonov, you must come too. You
have been assigned to the story.... Begin: 'Ivan Shukhov so
worships his country that he has the words. "I love the Union
of Soviet Socialist Republics" tattooed on his mighty arms.'

SEMYONOV: [*Startled*] But he hasn't.

PRISIPKIN: He will! [*Exit PRISIPKIN, VELIKOVSKY and
ABULADZE. Blackout—apart from the area around SEMYO-
NOV's desk.*]

SEMYONOV: [*In soliloquy*] Know what Prisipkin calls me,
behind my back? Dungman! Twenty years I've spent, shovel-
ling shit for him and his kind—to stop people smelling the
truth.... [*Glancing round.*] Get this: I'm doing a bit on the
side, see—the real, dung-free history of post-imperial Russia.
Purges, show trials, assassinations, labour camps, I've got the
lot—transcripts, affidavits, medical reports.... It's the ultim-
ate scoop! It'll rank me with the all-time greats Thucydides,
St Matthew, Norman Mailer.... I tell you, sometimes I envy
those Western scribes and their free Press. Know what I
dream about? Bringing down governments, righting wrongs,
exposing prostitution rackets, sodomy in the Navy, that sort
of thing.... I'm only human. Wouldn't mind an ounce of the
glory. Let's face it: I wouldn't even mind an electric typewriter.... But I'm no martyr. So I do as I'm told...till things

change. I've got my story locked away in little boxes—buried up and down the country, in the forests. Now and again I send a box to people I can trust: Semyonov's 'Unofficial History of Revolutionary Russia'—taking root in the Motherland! One day it'll burst into bloom.... One day...I ask you: can I beat the system on my own? [*Exit SEMYONOV. Blackout.*]

SCENE FOUR

In the darkness, a few bars of the national anthem are heard again. On-screen, a hospital interior—row on row of beds. Stage lights come up, revealing medical screens, surrounding a single bed: beside them, saluting, rather ridiculously, the COMMITTEE in line abreast. Music cuts. ABULADZE and VELIKOVSKY leap into action, folding back the screens to left and right of the bed —upon which are now seen IVAN and NATASHA, covered only by a sheet, making love. ABULADZE and VELIKOVSKY resume their positions in line. The lovers are quite unaware—until PRIS-IPKIN coughs (as considerately as he can). On the bed, action ceases; two heads turn towards the COMMITTEE. All at once, with a cry of alarm, IVAN leaps backwards off the bed, clutching the top sheet to his waist to cover his nakedness. NATASHA sits bolt upright, frantically pulling her dress down over her legs.
PRISIPKIN: [*To VELIKOVSKY*] Tell him to stand easy or something. [*NATASHA giggles.*]
VELIKOVSKY: [*Yelling*] You heard the man!
IVAN: Phew! [*NATASHA hurriedly fastens the front of her dress. Now, a white-coated and very pompous HOSPITAL SUPER-INTENDENT rushes on-stage, wringing his hands.*]
SUPERINTENDENT: [*To the COMMITTEE*] A thousand pardons, comrades! I wasn't expecting you so soon.
IVAN: [*Grumpily, under his breath*] Me neither.
SUPERINTENDENT: Be quiet, Shukhov. And stop dithering about like that. You're supposed to be resting. [*NATASHA bursts out laughing. IVAN tries to wrap the sheet round his waist.*] What, may I ask, is this woman doing in your bed?
IVAN: [*Deeply pained*] Nothing much.
SUPERINTENDENT: Nothing! [*Pointing at IVAN's groin.*] You call that nothing?
IVAN: Hardly bloody started. [*More giggling from NATASHA.*]
SUPERINTENDENT: [*Calling out*] Shagradov! [*Then to the COMMITTEE.*] Humble apologies, comrades. Most irregular! Shagradov! I must have an explanation! [*Enter Deputy Superintendent SHAGRADOV, hesitantly, stage left.*] Ah,

19

Shagradov, why is this woman in Shukhov's bed?

SHAGRADOV: Instructions, sir.

SUPERINTENDENT: [*Taken aback*] Instructions? Whose instructions?

PRISIPKIN: The President's.

SUPERINTENDENT: Ah, yes—yes, of course...the President's instructions.

PRISIPKIN: You were told to give the patient Shukhov everything he wished... [*The SUPERINTENDENT is flabbergasted.*] If only all one's orders were pursued with such...imagination!

SUPERINTENDENT: [*Graciously*] Thank you, comrade. We do our best.... Er, that will be all, Shagradov. [*Exit, disgruntled, SHAGRADOV. All this while, ABULADZE has been walking around IVAN, examining him through a monocle. To avoid him, IVAN adjusts and readjusts his sheet.*]

ABULADZE: Remarkable! Truly remarkable.... [*PRISIPKIN turns to NATASHA.*]

PRISIPKIN: And you must be Natasha.... Don't fret my child. There's nothing to be ashamed of. [*The SUPERINTENDENT helps NATASHA off the bed—she clutching her dress around her.*] I gather you wish to be a nurse.... See to that, will you, Superintendent? Such devotion to the patient must be very rare. [*NATASHA, baffled, curtsies to PRISIPKIN. The SUPERINTENDENT, even more baffled, holds her arm to lead her out. PRISIPKIN takes out a pen and uses it, fastidiously, to pick up Natasha's knickers from beside the bed.*] Natasha.... Won't you be needing these? [*Blushing, NATASHA takes the knickers and kisses IVAN warmly.*]

NATASHA: [*Whispering*] Who are they?

IVAN: No idea.

NATASHA: I'll come back when they've gone. [*Escorted by the SUPERINTENDENT, she exits.*]

PRISIPKIN: [*Commandingly*] Comrade Shukhov! [*IVAN comes to some semblance of attention.*] We are here to present you with a medal for your bravery in the Sheremestvo mine disaster.... General! [*VELIKOVSKY steps forward with a medal on a ribbon. He fastens it to the front of the sheet. IVAN's eyes raised to heaven. VELIKOVSKY steps back, then embraces IVAN so forcefully that he falls on to the bed, with the general in his arms. The bed breaks beneath them, with a crash.*]

VELIKOVSKY: Aaagh! [*PRISIPKIN and ABULADZE drag VELIKOVSKY aside and help IVAN to his feet. The SUPERINTENDENT re-enters.*]

SUPERINTENDENT: Oh, not the bed.... [*Examining it.*] Last winter, I ordered thirty new beds: they sent me six hundredweight of surgical boots. There seems to be a bottleneck in beds.

VELIKOVSKY: [*Bawling*] Improvise, man!

SUPERINTENDENT: Improvise.... Yes. Yes.... Perhaps there'll be something in the rule-book.... Shagradov! [*He scoots off-stage. PRISIPKIN wags his head, sighs, and transfixes IVAN with a dangerous smile.*]

PRISIPKIN: [*Most formally*] Ivan D. Shukhov, Hero of all the Russias, do you love your country?

IVAN: [*Startled*] Yes.

PRISIPKIN: Are you a sincere revolutionary socialist?

IVAN: I think so.

PRISIPKIN: Prove it!

IVAN: [*Hesitant*] You mean—do I believe in justice and truth?

PRISIPKIN: Yes?

IVAN: Liberty, equality, fraternity...?

PRISIPKIN: Go on.

IVAN: [*Gabbling, a little desperate*] And the new world order based on the dictatorship of the proletariat?

PRISIPKIN: Splendid! We have a proposition to put to you.

VELIKOVSKY: You are to join the Red Army.

IVAN: I'm exempt!

PRISIPKIN: Ah, yes. Russia needs her miners, just as she needs her soldiers. But the Army doesn't want you to be a soldier, Comrade Shukhov, it wants you to be the strongest man in the world.

IVAN: [*Laughing it off*] I *am* the strongest man in the world!

PRISIPKIN: [*Irresistible*] You know that, comrade, and we know it, but does the world? You will have heard, no doubt, of the Olympic Games.

IVAN: Yes....

ABULADZE: [*Rhapsodizing*] The grace and power of the human body at the peak of its performance....

PRISIPKIN: Quite.... Who was your boyhood hero, Ivan? Let me guess.... The mighty lifter, Zhabotinsky!

IVAN: [*Warming to the theme*] Yes--an' Lucis, the javelin thrower, an' the wrestler, Medved, an' Shakhlin, the gymnast—

PRISIPKIN: All of them, giants of their generations, Soviet Olympic champions. And you, too, we believe, can join the pantheon of your own heroes and become the archetype of the New Man—the man to stand at the peak of the evolutionary spiral, the man to surpass, in the flesh, the dream creatures of dead civilizations.... Homer's Achilles, Michelangelo's David... Ivan, we want you to win the Olympic Maxi-Weightlifting championship!

IVAN: Say that again.

PRISIPKIN: [*Patiently*] The Olympic Maxi-Weightlifting Championship.

IVAN: You must be joking. I don't know a weight from a wheelbarrer!

VELIKOVSKY: Hence the Army. We have the very best coaching facilities.

IVAN: Suppose I don't want to join the Army...?

VELIKOVSKY: [*Blustering again*] Not want to join the Army!

IVAN: What about my mother?

PRISIPKIN: We'll look after her.

IVAN: An' Natasha?

PRISIPKIN: [*Suavely*] Comrade Shukhov, please do not feel under any obligation. The choice is yours.... I have here a personal message from the President. May I read it?

IVAN: [*Overawed*] Yes.

PRISIPKIN: [*Reading*] 'My dear Ivan'—hear that?—'My dear Ivan, congratulations on your heroic feet'... [*Expostulating*] Feet! [*Spelling it out.*] F-e-e-t! [*Passionately*] Lunacharsky, wer't thou living at this hour! [*IVAN looks blank. PRISIPKIN recovers himself.*] Ahem! 'Dear Ivan, da-da da-da...it is vital to the cause of Russian socialism and the global revolution that you become the strongest man in the world. Signed: the President.' There you are, a personal invitation to glory! How many men receive such an honour? Not one in ten million. And none receives it twice.... Think of your father, Ivan, and your brother, your uncles, who all died for Russia. Remember them. As a patriot, you cannot refuse—can you? [*Pause*]

IVAN: [*Firmly*] No.

PRISIPKIN: Good.... One more thing: your tattoos—they must be changed to 'I love the Union of Soviet Socialist Republics'.

IVAN: [*Unsure whether it's serious*] My arms aren't long enough.

PRISIPKIN: Unlike Army regulations! [*PRISIPKIN claps his hands. Two SOLDIERS enter, with a uniform, boots and tape measure. They replace the screens around the broken bed, with IVAN hidden.*]

FIRST SOLDIER: [*From behind screens*] Chest: 120 centimetres.

SECOND SOLDIER: Check.

FIRST SOLDIER: Waist 87.5.

SECOND SOLDIER: Check.

FIRST SOLDIER: Inside leg 90.

SECOND SOLDIER: Check.

FIRST SOLDIER: Boot size eleven.

SECOND SOLDIER: Check.

FIRST SOLDIER: [*Poking his head through the screens*] Exact fit, sir.

PRISIPKIN: Excellent! [*As from a tannoy system, a village band*

plays loud military music. On-screen a village square. VILL-
AGERS and MINERS enter—including ALEXEI, BORIS,
NIKOLAI, etc. A dais is quickly erected for the COMMIT-
TEE; they climb on to it. NATASHA and MOTHER SHU-
KHOV are seen at the edge of the crowd. SEMYONOV also
enters, standing by the dais, notebook at the ready. The
music stops.]

PRISIPKIN: [*From the dais*] People of Sheremestvo: your village
will go down in history.... [*Cheers*] The story of your mine
rescue is on every lip, the name Ivan Shukhov on every tongue....
[*Cheers, applause.*] Brothers, your country, too, has need of
Shukhov's strength.... [*Cheers*] Brothers, Moscow calls!

ALL: Ooh!

PRISIPKIN: [*In full flow*] Today Ivan Shukhov joined the Red
Army... [*Cheers*] to prepare for the supreme Olympic weightlifting title.... [*Cheers*] And if he can hold the earth itself on
his great shoulders, how can he fail? [*Cheers*] Comrades, let
me present to you, Corporal Ivan Shukhov, the strongest man
in the world! [*The screens are whipped aside. IVAN is revealed, in a badly-fitting uniform and outsize cap, smiling awk-
wardly. More cheers, as the two SOLDIERS march him to the
front of the dais.*]

FIRST SOLDIER: By the right, mark time! Right wheel! Squad,
halt! [*Seeing NATASHA, as he marches clumsily round, IVAN
shrugs his shoulders, helplessly. NATASHA waves; MOTHER
SHUKHOV looks steely grim.*]

PRISIPKIN: Corporal Shukhov, [*Takes out his watch.*] in ten
minutes the train for the capital will pass through Sheremestvo.
Bid goodbye to your proud kinsfolk. When you return, it will
be as a hero, not just of Russia, but of mankind. [*The crowd
cheers; IVAN comes to embrace MOTHER SHUKHOV. He
kisses NATASHA. The COMMITTEE leaves the dais.*]
Time to go, Shukhov. Destiny waits!

FIRST SOLDIER: By the left, left turn---quick march! [*IVAN is
marched away, and the crowd follows. Suddenly, the stage
is empty, except for SEMYONOV, NATASHA and MOTHER
SHUKHOV.*]

NATASHA: When he's the strongest man in the world, what will
he want with me?

MOTHER SHUKHOV: What he always wanted, lass.... Any road,
never trust a committee! [*SEMYONOV approaches them,
notebook in hand.*]

SEMYONOV: Hello ladies---Basil Semyonov, correspondent of
Truth.

MOTHER SHUKHOV: Never get *Truth* 'ere, dear; distribution
problems, see?

23

SEMYONOV: Mamushka, open your heart! Tell me: how does a
   woman feel as her boy rides off into the sunset?
MOTHER SHUKHOV: What's the hurry? That train's always an
   hour late. [*She leads NATASHA slowly off-stage.*] Let's pray
   for 'im, love.
NATASHA: Pray, Mother Shukhov?
MOTHER SHUKHOV: Yes, pray! They can't wipe an old soul
   clean like a schoolroom blackboard.... When you've lost as
   much as I 'ave, you've gotta believe in something. [*NATA-
   SHA and MOTHER SHUKHOV exit. Meanwhile SEMYO-
   NOV is back at his desk. Light fades to a spot upon him.*]
SEMYONOV: [*Typing*] 'I give my child to Russia!' With these
   fine words Anna Shukhov today said goodbye to her hero
   son, Ivan, as he left his native village—a garland on his neck,
   his fiancée's kiss still fresh upon his cheek.... [*Blackout*]

SCENE FIVE

*Lights up. Fanfare. Six ATHLETES in red leotards, working at the
double, set the stage with gymnasium apparatus—and begin to
exercise. Centre-stage, on a mat, is a huge bar, with weights. On-
screen, the Olympic circles. SEMYONOV is seen, elbows on his
typewriter. Enter PRISIPKIN, with IVAN, in uniform, flanked
by ABULADZE and VELIKOVSKY.*
PRISIPKIN: [*Merrily*] Morning, Semyonov.
SEMYONOV: [*Bored*] Likewise.
PRISIPKIN: I take it this *is* the Palace of Physical Culture?
SEMYONOV: Room Thirteen.
ABULADZE: [*Proudly*] The Lenin Room.
VELIKOVSKY: Reserved for men of iron.
   [*Enter Coach KALOGRADOV, a big, square-shouldered man,
   in his mid-fifties, with red track-suit, close-cropped grey hair
   and sergeant-major's voice: he carries with him a stopwatch
   and whistle. Behind the coach comes DOCTOR ANDREYEV,
   a harassed, lugubrious gentleman, equipped with stethoscope
   and bag. Also the masseur, DIAGHILEV, a leering hunchback,
   with towels round his neck.*]
PRISIPKIN: What's that funny smell?
KALOGRADOV: Sweat! [*The COMMITTEE spin round, seeing
   KALOGRADOV for the first time: the six ATHLETES
   redouble their efforts.*]
PRISIPKIN: [*Shocked*] Ah, Coach Kalogradov! [*Grandly*] We
   bring you the strongest man in the world!
KALOGRADOV: About bleeding time! [*He surveys IVAN, with*
24

some derision.] So this is Mr Big....

PRISIPKIN: [*Bringing IVAN forward*] Corporal Ivan Shukhov, Hero of all the Russias!

KALOGRADOV: Kalogradov, Major—Coach, first class. [*They shake hands. SEMYONOV dances round in front of them with a small camera.*]

SEMYONOV: Say cheese! [*KALOGRADOV glares. As SEMYONOV snaps, IVAN smiles bravely.*]

PRISIPKIN: Don't be shy, Vanya. [*In mock amazement.*] Surely you've heard of the great Kalogradov, himself a former Olympic champion?

IVAN: [*Apologetic*] Sorry...

KALOGRADOV: Before his day!

PRISIPKIN: Well, it *was* 1948...

KALOGRADOV: And he wasn't even bleeding born!

PRISIPKIN: Er, yes.... Indeed.... Vanya, meet Doctor Andreyev, your personal physician, and Comrade Diaghilev, your masseur. [*IVAN smiles: ANDREYEV and DIAGHILEV bow.*] With the coach, they comprise the Committee to *Train* the Strongest Man in the World: I shall be chairman, ex officio.

KALOGRADOV: Which means he stays in his office while we do the bleeding work.... Nine months they've left us! Nine months, to turn a pitprop into gold.... Come on, corporal—jacket off: let's see what you can do. [*IVAN takes off his jacket—with DIAGHILEV's obtrusive help. The ATHLETES gather round. KALOGRADOV selects one of them.*] Gentlemen.... In modern weightlifting, there are two basic lifts: the jerk—so... [*The FIRST ATHLETE demonstrates, with much puffing and blowing.*] ...and the snatch—so.... [*Similarly*] To begin, we'll snatch 150 kilogrammes, right? When you're ready, sunshine. [*IVAN approaches the bar, bends, and clumsily, but easily, lifts. PRISIPKIN, VELIKOVSKY and ABULADZE applaud enthusiastically. SEMYONOV takes another picture. Sarcastically...*] You can put it down now, corporal.

IVAN: [*Feeling foolish*] Sorry. [*IVAN lowers the weight. Immediately, ANDREYEV and DIAGHILEV move in on him —ANDREYEV taking his pulse, sounding his heart, etc, DIAGHILEV massaging his chest, arms and so forth.*]

PRISIPKIN: There, what did we tell you?

VELIKOVSKY: Natural talent!

ABULADZE: Great beauty of form!

KALOGRADOV: [*Very deliberately*] Comrades, 150 kilos was the weight I snatched for the gold medal in 1948. These, comrades, are almost the 1980s—and in the 1980s, 150 kilos is puffed bleeding wheat. Don't talk to me about talent and —what was it?—beauty of form! Not any more. If your guy's gonna win, he's got to be a monster! Do I make myself clear?

PRISIPKIN, VELIKOVSKY, ABULADZE: [*In chorus*] Absolutely! [*They march over to IVAN.*]

PRISIPKIN: Au revoir, Corporal Shukhov...we leave you, I am sure, in capable hands.

ABULADZE: Good luck!

VELIKOVSKY: [*Saluting*] Russia expects!

[*PRISIPKIN, VELIKOVSKY and ABULADZE leave.*]

KALOGRADOV: Exit the top brass.... Arselickers unlimited! [*KALOGRADOV now calls to ANDREYEV.*] What's the verdict, doc?

ANDREYEV: Condition A1. [*DIAGHILEV, grinning his crazy grin, gives the thumbs-up sign.*]

KALOGRADOV: Proud of yourself, sunshine?

IVAN: [*Smiling*] Nothing to it.

KALOGRADOV: Smug bastard!

IVAN: [*Uncertain*] Sorry.

KALOGRADOV: Make up your bleeding mind: you're in the Army now.

IVAN: Yes, sir.

KALOGRADOV: Sir? Sir? What's all this 'sir' mularky? We're athletes here, not bleeding squaddies. You'll call me 'coach'. And let me tell you, athlete bleeding Shukhov, that was the lousiest bit of weightlifting it's ever been my misfortune to see.

IVAN: I did it, didn't I?

KALOGRADOV: Sure, you did it all right. But you did it all wrong. No method. No technique.

IVAN: Sorry, coach.

KALOGRADOV: [*Threateningly*] Oh, I'm gonna sort you out, Mr Bleeding Big: I'm gonna sort you out right here, right now.... [*KALOGRADOV blows his whistle. The ATHLETES add extra weights to the bar.*] One hundred and ninety kilos! We're waiting.

IVAN: [*Innocently*] Snatch or jerk?

KALOGRADOV: Corblimey! [*Mimicking*] Snatch or jerk? Snatch—you jerk! Snatch! [*IVAN hesitates. SEMYONOV picks up his camera. IVAN finally seizes the bar and raises it straight over his head; but he is off balance and falls to his knees. SEMYONOV takes another snap. KALOGRADOV, ANDREYEV, DIAGHILEV and the ATHLETES applaud excitedly.*] Fantastic! Bleeding fantastic! [*KALOGRADOV and DIAGHILEV lift IVAN to his feet.*]

IVAN: Sorry, coach.

KALOGRADOV: Sorry? Sunshine, that was the Olympic record. And you nearly made it in one. Maybe I can do something with you after all.

IVAN: [*Pleased but confused*] Thanks, coach.

KALOGRADOV: [*Exhortatory*] Shukhov, the maxiweight is a new category. It will be the Everest of the Moscow Olympics. And you are going to conquer it. Understand?

IVAN: [*Proudly*] Yes, coach.

KALOGRADOV: Comrade Diaghilev, get Mr Big kitted out, will you? [*DIAGHILEV leads IVAN off-stage. The ATHLETES also exit. To ANDREYEV...*] Few weeks' technique and toughening -then [*Meaningfully*] we'll see.... [*To SEMYO-NOV.*] Semyonov, stop skulking about and man your bleeding typewriter.... [*Dictating*] 'Today, exactly nine months before the Games, Corporal Shukhov commenced strict training. All Russia asks: will the "New Man" be born in time? Watch this space.' [*SEMYONOV has begun typing. Light comes down to a spot, on his desk.*]

SCENE SIX

Cut typing. Lights up. On-screen, the Olympic torch. Re-enter IVAN, in red leotard, with DIAGHILEV, to a lively Red Army marching tune. IVAN halts, centre-stage, running on the spot. Cut music. Now KALOGRADOV blows a loud blast on his whistle, signalling a hectic series of 'monthly' exercises, none lasting (with dialogue) more than thirty seconds.

KALOGRADOV: September, one! September, two! [*IVAN rushes across to the bicycle and begins pedalling furiously. Quick counts...*] Three, four, five, six, seven, eight.... Make it hurt, sunshine! If it doesn't hurt, you're not trying.... That's more like it. Pain! Greater the champion, greater the pain, eh Diaghilev? [*IVAN starts doing press-ups on the floor. Mocking...*] Oh good boy, good boy—gentleman always takes the weight on his elbows, eh Diaghilev? Push, sunshine—push back that pain barrier! Twenty eight, twenty nine, thirty! Rest! [*IVAN flops on to the stage. ANDREYEV and DIA-GHILEV begin their ministrations.*] Semyonov, take a bulletin. 'Month one: excellent progress.' [*SEMYONOV types the bulletin. Consulting his stopwatch...*] Ready, doctor?

ANDREYEV: Ready, coach. [*ANDREYEV and DIAGHILEV retreat. IVAN leaps up, running on the spot. KALOGRADOV blows the whistle.*]

KALOGRADOV: October! [*IVAN picks up a pair of dumb-bells and begins raising them, running on the spot. Quick counts...*] One, two, three, four, five, six, seven... [*As IVAN lifts,*

SEMYONOV snaps around him like a fashion photographer.]
Semyonov, put away that camera and get me Prisipkin on the
phone. [*SEMYONOV goes to the desk and dials. IVAN drops
the dumb-bells and turns now to a set of chest expanders.*]
Fifteen, sixteen, seventeen, eighteen, nineteen.... [*SEMYO-
NOV holds the telephone to KALOGRADOV.*] Tell him to
get over here, right away, savvy? [*He picks up a medicine ball:
IVAN lies on the floor: KALOGRADOV throws the ball at
his stomach; IVAN grimaces, brave and silent.*] Hurt, did it?
Let's make it hurt some more. You're as slack as an old
priest's bum.... [*He throws again.*] Twenty-nine, thirty, thirty-
one! Rest! [*ANDREYEV and DIAGHILEV rush to IVAN.
The ATHLETES return and set new weights on the bar.
Enter PRISIPKIN.*] Ah, Comrade Prisipkin.

PRISIPKIN: [*Flustered, seeing IVAN prone*] Is anything wrong?

KALOGRADOV: Quite the reverse. Corporal Shukhov is just
about to bury the Olympic record, aren't you sunshine?

IVAN: [*Radiant with confidence*] Yes, coach.

KALOGRADOV: Condition, doctor?

ANDREYEV: A1 plus. [*DIAGHILEV gives thumbs-up. IVAN
rises, prepares. The ATHLETES stand back to watch....
IVAN is now a technically proficient lifter; he lifts success-
fully, with superb strength, at both snatch and jerk.*]

KALOGRADOV: [*Announcing*] Snatch—210 kilos!

IVAN: Aaah!
[*SEMYONOV takes a picture. IVAN puts down the bar. The
ATHLETES reset the weights.*]

KALOGRADOV: Jerk—260 kilos!

IVAN: [*As before*] Aaah! [*SEMYONOV again takes a picture.
ANDREYEV and DIAGHILEV attend to IVAN.*]

KALOGRADOV: Total: 470 kilos! 70 over the qualifying mark!
[*The ATHLETES applaud and exit.*]

PRISIPKIN: [*Rushing forward*] Congratulations, my dear
Shukhov—and still seven months to go. [*PRISIPKIN poses
exaggeratedly with IVAN for another of SEMYONOV's
snaps.*] Coach, you've worked wonders. I shall inform the
President immediately. It's his birthday, you know.... [*Aside,
to SEMYONOV.*] There's a dinner at the Kremlin. Wasn't
invited last year. [*PRISIPKIN is about to rush off-stage.
KALOGRADOV stops him.*]

PRISIPKIN: [*Annoyed*] What now?

KALOGRADOV: Victor! [*On-screen, appears the picture of a
massive black weightlifter.*] The negro! That's what! His
name's White—can you believe it? Abraham Lincoln bleeding
White! Alias 'Geronimo'. In short, comrades, the enemy.

IVAN: Whose enemy?

KALOGRADOV: Yours, sunshine. We've been saving him up for
    you. He's the American champion—the secret weapon of free
    enterprise. And he's just totalled 500 kilos. Come the Games,
    he'll have hit 560!
IVAN: [*In sheer disbelief*] Ballocks!
KALOGRADOV: Honest Injun! 560!...Let's face it, sunshine,
    you're not gonna be a patch on old Geronimo... [*Suggestively*]
    without the drugs.
IVAN: [*Bewildered*] Drugs? [*SEMYONOV is covertly trying to
    take notes.*]
PRISIPKIN: [*Sharply*] Notebooks away, Semyonov. [*SEMYONOV
    does as he's told.*]
IVAN: [*Recovering himself*] I'm not taking any drugs.
KALOGRADOV: [*Cruelly*] Don't see how you've much choice,
    sunshine. I'd say you were near your natural peak. You've put
    on about 30 kilos. To whip Geronimo, you'll need another
    100. Where are they coming from, eh? Well, I'll tell you.
    Extra bodyweight! Fat! Blubber! Flesh! That's what you need,
    sunshine. Take a look at the enemy. Go on, take a good look....
    Now, what's the difference...? You're taller than him, you're
    fitter than him—dammit, you're better than him. But he's got
    the pudding, sunshine—the extra black pudding. And there's
    muscle in it: he's got the muscle-power. And it didn't grow by
    magic.... [*Calling*] Victor! [*On-screen the picture changes, to
    show a younger, skinnier, neatly-muscled negro, full-length,
    naked—as in the first picture of IVAN.*] Geronimo—two years
    back.... Pretty, isn't he? All firm and rampant, like you—the
    bastard.... Victor! [*The picture reverts.*] Behold—the same
    guy...built by drugs!
PRISIPKIN: [*Unctuously*] Truly, horrible!
IVAN: I feel sorry for him.
KALOGRADOV: To win, you'll have to bleeding hate him.
IVAN: Hate him?
PRISIPKIN: Yes, Shukhov! Hate in him the society that has driven
    him to such self-mutilation!
IVAN: But you want to do the same to me.
KALOGRADOV: No, no, nothing like that, sunshine. [*Avuncular
    again.*] Just add a bit here and there, eh, doctor?
ANDREYEV: Er, yes, coach.
KALOGRADOV: A controlled experiment, eh, doctor?
PRISIPKIN: Precisely.
KALOGRADOV: When it's all over, a few spells in the steam bath
    and your own mother wouldn't know the difference.
IVAN: You're not experimenting on me.
PRISIPKIN: [*Silkily*] Perhaps if the doctor described the drugs
    involved...

KALOGRADOV: Because it just so happens he has a bottle in his bag.

ANDREYEV: [*Touchily*] They're called steraboloids.

PRISIPKIN: Ah, yes, steraboloids. Correct me, doctor, if I'm wrong, but weren't they used to treat survivors of the Nazi death camps after the war?

KALOGRADOV: Male hormones, sunshine: give you a protein boost to build new muscles in training. Geronimo's got the stuff running out of his ears.

IVAN: It's not right!

KALOGRADOV: Snag is, sunshine, it works. Would you rather play fair and lose?

IVAN: Maybe I'd rather not play at all.

PRISIPKIN: Impossible!

KALOGRADOV: Too late to back out now.

PRISIPKIN: We've checked, Ivan: you're the one man in the world who could beat Geronimo.

IVAN: [*Passionately*] It wouldn't be me: it'd be the drugs. Where do I come in?

PRISIPKIN: On the victory rostrum, in the national stadium, for the glory of Mother Russia!

KALOGRADOV: Grow up, sunshine. This isn't ancient bleeding Greece. Everybody's on drugs nowadays.... What good's the second strongest man in the world? It's ends and means, sunshine—ends and bleeding means.

IVAN: How did I get into all this?

PRISIPKIN: Quite simple really.

IVAN: [*Exploding*] Yes, to you it is—'cos you knew, didn't you?

PRISIPKIN: Vanya, my dear chap!

IVAN: You knew all the time. Back home in Sheremestvo, when you were callin' me a hero, you knew then.

PRISIPKIN: [*Backing away*] Ivan, I assure you...

IVAN: You knew all about the black man. You planned the drugs all along, didn't you? 'Cos you thought I'd never beat him.

PRISIPKIN: [*Backing further*] Corporal Shukhov, I...

IVAN: [*Irresistible*] You lied to me.

PRISIPKIN: No! Aaaah! [*His denial turns to a cry of horror as IVAN grabs him in a fearsome half-Nelson.*]

IVAN: Didn't you?

PRISIPKIN: Ye-e-e-es! Coach, help!

KALOGRADOV: [*Amused, laconic*] Round the bleeding bend, are you, sunshine? That's the First Deputy Minister of Sport you've got there. Wouldn't hurt him, if I were you.

IVAN: [*Innocently*] I'm not hurting him. I'm just showing him how strong I am.

PRISIPKIN: [*Discomfited*] Corporal, please—you're a Colossus!

IVAN: I don't need any drugs, do I?

PRISIPKIN: Corporal, be sensible...aaah! [*IVAN suddenly exerts the full-Nelson.*]

IVAN: I can win the title just as I am.... Can't I?

PRISIPKIN: Yes, Corporal—just as you are!

IVAN: All I need is some heavier training.... Don't I?

PRISIPKIN: Yes, Corporal—heavier training.... [*Begging*] Can I have my head back now? [*Roughly, IVAN releases PRISIP-KIN, who staggers dizzily. ANDREYEV and DIAGHILEV rush to minister to him. PRISIPKIN, horrified, pushes them aside, feeling his neck.*]

KALOGRADOV: [*Incensed*] This is mutiny! He should be court-martialled! [*SEMYONOV is secretly taking notes again. To SEMYONOV...*] Give me that book! [*He rips the notebook to shreds. To IVAN.*] ...Now look here, smart alec, I'm a major, see, and you're just a bleeding corporal. If I tell you to take drugs, you bleeding well take drugs. Andreyev'd stick 'em up your arse for breakfast, if I said so. [*ANDREYEV looks ashamed. IVAN turns, menacingly, back to PRISIPKIN.*]

PRISIPKIN: [*Desperately*] No, no, coach. Ivan is correct. We shouldn't compel him: his heart wouldn't be in the struggle... [*Regaining confidence and cunning.*] I...er...I propose a different experiment. Give the corporal two more months...

KALOGRADOV: Two more months!

PRISIPKIN: Then we can reconsider the matter of the...er...drugs. Does that seem fair, Corporal?

IVAN: [*Grateful*] Thank you, comrade.

KALOGRADOV: [*Getting the idea*] Waste of bleeding time!

PRISIPKIN: No, coach—it's the corporal's right. Let him use it. Let him work to the last ounce of strength, the last drop of blood, and, who knows, Russia may yet bring back the spirit of ancient Greece to the Olympic Games.... Is it a bargain, Shukhov?

IVAN: [*Enthusiastically*] Yes, comrade chairman. I'll not let you down.

PRISIPKIN: I trust not, Ivan, I trust not. [*Exit PRISIPKIN.*]

KALOGRADOV: All right, Mr Big, you asked for it—and you're bleeding well going to get it. Schedule Ten! [*With a blast on his whistle.*] Fingers crossed it doesn't kill you! [*On-screen, now, a Greek temple. Reprise of march tune. The ATHLETES re-enter, at the double, bringing body irons. To IVAN's horror, they fix the irons to his arms and legs—then exit.*] Ready, doctor?

ANDREYEV: [*Resigned*] Ready, coach.

KALOGRADOV: [*Blowing his whistle*] November, one! November, two! [*Straight away, IVAN starts knee-bends, with arms out-*

stretched.] Three, four, five, six... [*IVAN now switches to the 'hopak' dance—squatting down, arms folded, and thrusting forward his weighted legs in turn.*] Seventeen, eighteen, nineteen, twenty... [*IVAN moves to the weightlifting 'machine' and proceeds to do 'chin up' lifts on it—his head thrown back in pain.*] If Geronimo could see you now! Talk about sweating blood! Should've taken your medicine, sunshine, like a good boy. [*IVAN now staggers across to the bicycle and begins pedalling.*] Twenty-seven, twenty-eight, twenty-nine, thirty. Rest! [*IVAN collapses forward on to the handlebars. ANDREYEV and DIAGHILEV rush across and lift him off on to the floor to carry out their tests and massage.*] Aches, does it? Not surprised. Anything worth having in this world aches like hell.

ANDREYEV: You're pushing him too hard.

KALOGRADOV: That's his fault.... [*Calling out.*] Semyonov! Bulletin! 'Month three: excellent progress.' [*As SEMYONOV finishes typing, KALOGRADOV blows his whistle.*] On your feet, sunshine! Got a surprise for you. [*Re-enter the ATHLETES. IVAN stands now, while a large wooden beam—like a pit prop—is fastened across his neck and along his outstretched arms. The ATHLETES exit. Consulting his stopwatch...*] December! [*Immediately, IVAN—yoked and weighted—starts to run round the stage.*] One, two, three, four, five, six.... Recognize that beam, sunshine? Had it shipped in special—from Sheremestvo.... Bleeding heroes! [*As KALOGRADOV laughs mockingly, IVAN stumbles. KALOGRADOV takes up the count again. IVAN struggles on. Emphatically...*] Twelve, thirteen, fourteen, fifteen.... [*IVAN falls. ANDREYEV and DIAGHILEV rush across and begin unfastening the yoke.*]

ANDREYEV: It's too much!

KALOGRADOV: Let me worry about that.... [*Calling out.*] Semyonov, get the chairman over here! [*Now, IVAN, lying flat on his stomach, has weights piled on his back—and must do press-ups despite them. Meanwhile, SEMYONOV is busy on the telephone.*] Chin up, sunshine—nearly there!... Eighteen, nineteen, twenty, twenty-one.... [*IVAN is gasping in agony. KALOGRADOV comes to stand over him.*]

ANDREYEV: It's torture.

KALOGRADOV: Naaah! S'training—isn't it, sunshine? Hear that? Pain! Pure bleeding pain! He gets the medal, I dish out the pain. [*KALOGRADOV now sits on IVAN's back. IVAN cries out—but must continue the press-ups...slowly, excruciatingly. Grinning...*] Twenty-eight, twenty-nine, thirty, thirty-one. Happy New Year! [*Whistle-blast. The ATHLETES re-enter to set more weights on the bar. ANDREYEV and DIAGHILEV rush across to the exhausted IVAN, taking off the irons, etc. Enter PRISIPKIN.*] Ah, comrade chairman—just completing our preparations.

PRISIPKIN: So I see.... [*Decisively*] Corporal Shukhov, the two months are up. Are you ready? [*Painfully, IVAN gets to his feet.*]

KALOGRADOV: Ready as he'll ever be—Mother Nature's way.

PRISIPKIN: Corporal, do you agree? Normal training can take you no further?

IVAN: [*Grimly determined*] Yes.

PRISIPKIN: Then I call you to the test! [*The ATHLETES stand back.*]

KALOGRADOV: Target: the enemy's last known lift....

PRISIPKIN: Agreed?

IVAN: Yes.

KALOGRADOV: [*Gloating*] 310 kilos--jerk!

ANDREYEV: It's impossible!

KALOGRADOV: Course it's impossible—except for Geronimo. [*Bowing, mockingly, KALOGRADOV ushers IVAN to the bar.*] Know what he calls you, sunshine? Whitey! Piddling little whitey, weak as maiden's water, he says, like all Commies. Bleeding racialist! I wouldn't take it, sunshine not from a nigger, I wouldn't—bleeding buck nigger! Squeeze him, sunshine: let's hear them black pips squeak. Squeeze that bar, sunshine, give it some hate. Strangle the bastard! [*IVAN prepares himself, stands before the bar—he bends and, with an enormous effort, raises it to his chest and holds it there, straining.*] Come on, sunshine, lift it—lift the bleeding thing! [*IVAN cannot make the final push.*] More hate, Shukhov! Where's the hate? More hate, man!

IVAN: [*His face contorted*] I can't.

PRISIPKIN: For your mother, Ivan—for Natasha.

IVAN: [*Shaking his head*] I can't.

PRISIPKIN: For your country, then—for Russia.

IVAN: [*With a long cry*] I can't!
[*The ATHLETES, too, are roaring their encouragement. But IVAN cracks, drops the bar and falls to his knees. On the whistle, the ATHLETES exit. PRISIPKIN and KALOGRADOV exchange satisfied glances.*]

PRISIPKIN: [*Approaching*] Ivan, my boy, you were magnificent. You did all that a mortal can do.

IVAN: I bloody lost!

PRISIPKIN: Lost? Corporal, your progress in four months is unequalled in the entire history of weightlifting.

IVAN: Not enough!

33

PRISIPKIN: My dear chap, it's more than enough. With continued
   training and Doctor Andreyev's help, your victory is assured.
   As a patriot, your duty is now clear—is it not?
IVAN: [*Accepting the inevitable*] Yes, comrade.
PRISIPKIN: The doctor has the dosages prepared...?
ANDREYEV: Yes, comrade chairman. [*IVAN, still on his knees,
   is shaking his head in exhaustion, despair.*]
IVAN: What's going to happen to me?
PRISIPKIN: [*Triumphantly*] You're going to become the strong-
   est man in the world!
IVAN: Am I?
KALOGRADOV: [*Brutally*] Andreyev had better get his spunk
   specimens first.
PRISIPKIN: [*Coughing*] Ah, yes... [*Taking a set of pink forms
   from his pocket.*] Er, Corporal Shukhov, there is one matter...
   I have here, in triplicate, permission to expend sperm on
   behalf of the State, all properly endorsed by the Ministry of
   Health.... Would you, er, care to sign? [*PRISIPKIN holds out
   the papers.*]
IVAN: [*Unbelieving*] Pardon? [*KALOGRADOV grabs open
   ANDREYEV's bag, takes out a large test tube and waves it in
   front of IVAN's nose.*]
KALOGRADOV: Imagine, sunshine—at your natural peak! What
   a vintage!
IVAN: [*Crying out*] It's my body!
PRISIPKIN: Of course, Ivan, you lucky fellow. But is it yours to
   use as you will? Such a body is a privilege. It belongs to your
   family, your forebears, who helped build it: it belongs to
   Mother Russia, who reared it: it belongs to the future, through
   the children you create—and may you create many children,
   Ivan, in your own magnificent image: you and your Natasha....
   But Natasha is a personal fancy, Ivan, and your body is too
   valuable for personal fancies.... Think of Volubskaya, the
   sprinter, or Tallich, the discus-thrower.... Yes, Ivan, think of
   Tallich. Were your seed placed within her, oh what a giant we
   should see, what a gift to your country, to the world, to the
   science of human possibility! [*IVAN is defeated. DIAGHILEV
   helps him to his feet. KALOGRADOV gives him the test tube.
   PRISIPKIN gives him the papers. DIAGHILEV leads IVAN
   from the stage. ANDREYEV follows, with KALOGRADOV
   and PRISIPKIN. SEMYONOV is left alone, at his desk,
   typing.*]
SEMYONOV: 'The science of human possibility'! [*He tears the
   paper from his typewriter and, walking round the desk, rolls
   up the great screed of bulletins.*] What's wrong? Didn't expect me to speak for him, did you? I've told you: I know the

score. Cynic to the core. Them as don't like it can always show me the door. Long as they don't break my jaw: might need it one day—for laying down the law.... Not to speak of the Games. I'm to be Russia's top commentator, see. Me—Basil Semyonov, the eyes and ears of the nation! Best polish up the old prose, eh—paint out the grey hairs, get some priority dentures, fix the wart on my nose. Let's face it: this is the big time! They might even raise me a quarter, put whisky in my water, give me a poke at the editor's daughter—and I tell you, that's happened to shorter blokes than me! Makes you sore, does it? Sticks in your craw? Sorry to be such a bore. In this war, comrades, you've gotta keep in your oar. If you feel sick, don't forget to lick up the floor! [*SEMYONOV exits, with his scroll, throwing a last, winning smile at the audience.*]

SCENE SEVEN

On-screen, a modern Olympic stadium, with the legend, 'MOSCOW 1980'. Pools of light, for various acting areas. Rear-stage, a podium, with steps; centre-stage, the weightlifting bar and mat; down-stage, left, MOTHER SHUKHOV and NATASHA watching a large television set. Loudly, an Olympic fanfare sounds. Then the voice of SEMYONOV, commentator.

SEMYONOV: [*Voice off*] People of the Soviet Union, welcome to the twenty-fifth Olympiad. Welcome once more to the battlefield of sport—a battlefield already hallowed by revolutionary victories. [*On-screen now, a sequence of stills depicting Soviet Olympic triumphs.*]

MOTHER SHUKHOV: [*Hunched on her chair, wrapped in a shawl*] That's the little liar from *Truth*, isn't it? Flyin' high, now, on Vanya's shoulders...just like I dreamed.

NATASHA: What did you dream, Mother Shukhov?

MOTHER SHUKHOV: The dark dream, child. Every night since they took him, I've seen my Ivan stretched out in a bare, black tree, an' the tree creatures fastenin' on him—jackdaws, owls, old black corbies...an' that Semyonov, with the cigar, he's one of 'em- he's the vulture on my Ivan's back!

NATASHA: Vanya wouldn't let anyone hurt him.... Give me your hand.... [*She takes MOTHER SHUKHOV's hand.*] You're shivering! Come on, forget the dream. Watch for your son. [*SEMYONOV is heard again, excitedly building up the commentary tension.*]

SEMYONOV: Today, comrades, is the day of all Olympic days. Today, in the eyes of the watching world, Moscow will crown

35

the strongest man on earth! [*Again, a loud fanfare. On-screen, a huge Socialist Realist portrait of the revolutionary worker. A hullabaloo, off-stage, left. Enter ALEXEI, NIKOLAI, BORIS, DIMITROV and BRODSKY, carrying chairs and vodka bottles, singing lustily.*]

MINERS: When Vanya Shukhov lifts that bar, he's gonna shift a ton! Oh Vanya, Vanya...

ALEXEI: Just in time, are we?

NATASHA: Shhh!

NIKOLAI: [*Finger to lips*] Shhh.

MINERS: [*Drunkenly*] Shhhhh! [*They burst into laughter and sit down.*]

ALEXEI: Come to wish 'im luck!

MOTHER SHUKHOV: There's no luck in a long bottle an' never was.

ALEXEI: Colliers, present...arms! [*The MINERS jump to attention, bottles raised.*] To Ivan Shukhov!

MINERS: [*Loudly*] To Ivan Shukhov! [*They flop noisily to their chairs.... MOTHER SHUKHOV tightens the shawl around her. Enter, down-stage, right, with stand microphone and cigar —SEMYONOV.*]

SEMYONOV: Live, comrades, from the Supreme Citadel of Socialist Sport, Soviet Television brings you the first contest for the new Olympic Maxiweightlifting title. Introducing on your right, the Yankee Champion, Abraham Lincoln White, known in the bar-bell business as Geronimo, a descendant of slaves, son of a farmhand from Phallus, Dixieland—aiming now to reap gold for imperialism. [*On-screen the face of GERONIMO—loose, fleshy, but smiling and confident.*]

MOTHER SHUKHOV: [*Crossing herself*] Lord save us!

MINERS: Boo!

NATASHA: Oh, Vanya! [*SEMYONOV's commentary rises half an octave in pride.*]

SEMYONOV: And on my left, comrades, from Sheremestvo, south of Krasnodar, son of the revolution, great white hope of the proletariat, Ivan Shukhov! [*On-screen, IVAN's face —much fatter round the cheeks, jaw and neck, pouchy under the eyes. MOTHER SHUKHOV jumps from her chair, pointing at the television. NATASHA, too, rises.*]

MOTHER SHUKHOV: [*Crying out*] Is that my son?

ALEXEI: By 'ell, woman, you should know!

NATASHA: [*Quietly*] What have they done to him?

NIKOLAI: Made 'im bigger, lass.

BORIS: Given 'im bodyweight.

BRODSKY: Extra bodyweight.

DIMITROV: Must 'ave bodyweight!

BORIS: S'part of the game.

MOTHER SHUKHOV: [*Apocalyptically*] I see evil done upon
my son's body! [*Shocked silence. NATASHA persuades
MOTHER SHUKHOV to sit down.*]

SEMYONOV: The scene is set. Before you, the only two men
who even qualified for this titanic event. Truly, theirs is a
duel of giants. So far, not a kilogramme conceded, not a
gramme. It's more than flesh and blood can stand!
[*MOTHER SHUKHOV leaps to her feet.*]

MOTHER SHUKHOV: Yea, on the flesh of my child are your
foul crimes committed!

ALEXEI: Gerraway, woman—few steam baths an' he'll be his old
self again.

NATASHA: [*Drawing MOTHER SHUKHOV back to her seat*]
There aren't any steam baths in Sheremestvo.

BORIS: Sheremestvo, is it? If Vanya wins, there'll be no more
Sheremestvo.

NATASHA: [*Turning on him*] He belongs here!

BORIS: He's a flamin' hero: he belongs in Moscow.

MOTHER SHUKHOV: And if he loses?

NATASHA: Don't think of it--don't even think of it!
[*SEMYONOV resumes his commentary.*]

SEMYONOV: Experts say the next lift will be decisive: 320 kilos,
jerk—a staggering 60 kilos over the Olympic record. Comrades,
Geronimo goes first. Am I correct? Does humanity hold its
very breath? The great negro bends to the bar. [*Suddenly
sharper.*] I think we have 'lift-off'—yes, we have 'lift-off'....
Now, can he thrust for the sky? I don't think so. Geronimo
can't make it. [*Elated*] The body buckles, the bar falls.
America is vanquished!
[*The MINERS leap up in excitement, waving arms and bottles.
But SEMYONOV's commentary breaks through once more.*]
Oh, but what a tragedy is here? Comrades, the negro has gone
berserk! He tears his hair, comrades, and runs against the
walls: his coaches, he hurls them aside, like dolls: his head,
comrades, he bangs it on the floor—bangs it, bangs his head.
See how it takes a dozen men to grapple him, and doctors,
with their needles, to subdue him.
[*The gleeful MINERS grasp something is wrong.*]

MOTHER SHUKHOV: The poor man. The poor, poor man.

ALEXEI: Poor man bedamned!

NIKOLAI: S'tough at the top, widow-woman.

BORIS: Hadn't got what it takes.

MOTHER SHUKHOV: God help him!

SEMYONOV: Comrades, a woeful sight.... Such was America's
need to win: such was the athlete's desperation. Surely,

37

nothing can stop Ivan Shukhov now!

ALEXEI: Come on, Vanya!

NIKOLAI, BORIS: Vanya Shukhov!

MINERS: [*All taking up the chant*] Vanya Shukhov! Vanya Shukhov!

[*Enter, IVAN, body clearly much bulkier now, in his lifting gear. Slowly, he prepares himself.*]

SEMYONOV: [*Breathless*] Can any man be so strong...?

[*IVAN bends to the bar, then, with a lunge, lifts it to his chest.*]

ALEXEI: Lift, Vanya!

DIMITROV: Lift it, man!

NATASHA: Please, Vanya—please, please....

[*IVAN raises the weight above his head and holds it there.*]

IVAN: [*Howling*] Brodsky!

[*IVAN drops the bar, bows gravely and exits.*]

SEMYONOV: He's done it! He's done it! Ivan Shukhov is the New Man! [*Screen-picture changes to the Russian flag, with hammer and sickle. On-stage, everything erupts. The MINERS, cheering and shouting, seize NATASHA and MOTHER SHUKHOV and dance with them wildly.... All at once, the celebrations are stopped by SEMYONOV's ringing voice.*] People of the Soviet Union, meet the Strongest Man in the World!

[*Re-enter, IVAN—track-suited now, head swathed in towels. The MINERS, NATASHA and MOTHER SHUKHOV crowd back round the television set. SEMYONOV continues, grandly...*] Corporal Shukhov, I bring you the congratulations of your countrymen.

IVAN: [*Smiling, shyly*] Thank you, comrade.

SEMYONOV: Tell me—the whole world will want to hear—what was that great cry you uttered at the moment of crisis?

IVAN: [*Matter-of-fact*] Brodsky.

SEMYONOV: [*Baffled*] Brodsky?

[*The MINERS roar with laughter.*]

IVAN: Semyon Brodsky. He's a miner I was trapped with in a pitfall. His lungs are so black you could polish 'em.

SEMYONOV: And this Comrade Brodsky was your inspiration?

IVAN: [*Quietly*] Yes.... I did it for Brodsky.

[*Across-stage, everyone is clapping BRODSKY on the back, sending him into a paroxysm of coughing.*]

ALEXEI: Hear that?

NIKOLAI: He did it for Brodsky!

[*Through the noise, SEMYONOV pursues the interview further.*]

SEMYONOV: Bravo! Truly a people's champion! And could I

ask: what are your plans now?

IVAN: [*Decidedly*] To get married.

[*Round the set, a shout of glee—with kisses and cuddles for NATASHA.*]

ALEXEI: And about time, eh, lass?

SEMYONOV: Who's the lucky girl?

IVAN: [*Blushing*] Natasha Andreyevna Konstantin.

SEMYONOV: Of your own village—Sheremestvo?

IVAN: Yes.

SEMYONOV: Well, I have a surprise for you. In honour of your patriotic efforts, the Government has installed colour television in every house in Sheremestvo. [*IVAN smiles and waves, happily. The television group waves merrily back —at the set. IVAN and SEMYONOV exit.*]

MINERS: Good old Vanya!

ALEXEI: There, widow-woman, aren't you proud of 'im?

MOTHER SHUKHOV: Proud? Yes, I'm proud. He's a good boy, my Ivan. But do they have steam-baths in Moscow, that's what I'm thinking. [*Everyone laughs.*]

BORIS: In Moscow, they live in their flamin' baths!

NIKOLAI: Aye, sunken ones, wi' marble tiles.

DIMITROV: Namore tin tubs an' pit muck for Vanya!

BRODSKY: Nay, he'll 'ave perfumed soap.

NIKOLAI: An' lambs-wool towels.

ALEXEI: An' a maid to scrub his back, eh, lass?

NATASHA: [*Gaily*] Jealousy'll get you nowhere.

BORIS: [*Still half-serious*] You'll see.

NATASHA: I can't wait!

[*Fanfare sounds. The group round the television is drawn to a semblance of attention. Again, IVAN enters, climbing the steps to the podium. SEMYONOV's commentary voice is heard, as sound-off.*]

SEMYONOV: [*Hushed tones*] Owing to the indisposition of his one rival, Ivan Shukhov, Hero of all the Russias, stands alone, on his native soil, a Colossus above men, wearing the golden medal of glory. [*IVAN turns to face the audience and stands to attention. Solemnly...*] Soviet people, witness—the revolution incarnate: the inevitable made flesh!

[*The Soviet national anthem.... Kissing his medal, IVAN gives the clenched fist salute. Before the television, the MINERS and NATASHA salute similarly. MOTHER SHUKHOV weeps.*]

ACT TWO

SCENE ONE

Darkness. Music—Tchaikovsky's 'Romeo and Juliet' love theme. On-screen, the Soviet flag, with the caption 'Pleas, Protests and Petitions'. Cut picture and music.
Lights up—revealing a large, ornate, four-poster bed, with curtains drawn. The bed itself is brightly lit, the rest of the stage subdued. On-screen: a Moscow city-scape, river in the distance.... Silence. Suddenly, the curtains are pulled back. IVAN and NATASHA are in bed, he in striped pyjamas, she in a nightdress. Both are sitting up, arms clasped round their knees. IVAN's extra bodyweight has disappeared.

IVAN: Whadya do that for?
NATASHA: We've got to get up sometime, love.
IVAN: Why?
NATASHA: Because we've been in bed for a week. [*IVAN gazes stonily ahead.*] Vanya, please—I keep telling you: it doesn't matter.
IVAN: Course it matters.
NATASHA: [*Shaking her head*] No!
IVAN: [*Emphatically*] It matters to me. [*He reaches up, pulls the cord: the curtains close.*]
NATASHA: [*Wildly*] Stop it! Stop it! [*The curtains swing open again.*]
IVAN: Sorry. [*He puts an arm around her, holds her.*]
NATASHA: It matters to me, too—you know that.
IVAN: Mmmmm.
NATASHA: But it's not everything.... [*IVAN takes away his arm.*] We love each other, don't we? It'll be all right again, you'll see.... Vanya!
IVAN: [*Awefully*] There's something wrong with me.
NATASHA: Don't say that!
IVAN: There must be: it's never happened before.
NATASHA: [*Tartly*] With Mishkina, you mean.... Or that blonde from the tyre factory.... Or your cousin Sonya.
IVAN: Who told you about my cousin Sonya?
NATASHA: [*Laughing*] Your mother.
IVAN: My mother!
40

NATASHA: She told me about your Aunty Grusha as well.

IVAN: That was years ago.

NATASHA: On the picnic, when your uncle fell asleep and she took you looking for squirrels....

IVAN: In the woods.

NATASHA: With bushy tails! [*Pause*] Was it all right with Aunty Grusha?

IVAN: [*Smugly*] What do *you* think?

NATASHA: [*Suggestive*] It was all right with us, too...wasn't it?

IVAN: [*Smiling ruefully*] Yeah.

NATASHA: You see.

IVAN: Till last Sunday.

NATASHA: Mmmmm...Maybe you just needed a rest...Maybe we... Maybe if... [*They kiss.... She reaches up and pulls the cord: the curtains close.... Silence. A doorbell rings. IVAN curses.*]

IVAN: Blast! Damn an' bloody blast!

NATASHA: Shh.

[*Pause. Doorbell rings again. NATASHA, puzzled, pops her head out of the curtains at the foot of the bed. IVAN yells out, from behind her.*]

IVAN: Go away! [*NATASHA climbs down through the curtains.*]

NATASHA: Better see. Might be the doctor.... [*Moving to stage left.*] Doctor Andreyev—we thought it might be you. [*Enter ANDREYEV, with medical bag—looking worried.*]

ANDREYEV: Oh dear, did you? Er, is your husband about?

NATASHA: [*Fastening her nightdress*] Yes, he's in bed.

ANDREYEV: Not poorly, I hope.... Perhaps I could call another time.

NATASHA: No, we were just getting up.... [*Calling*] Weren't we, Vanya?

IVAN: [*Behind curtain*] No!

NATASHA: [*Smiling—to ANDREYEV*] What day is it?

ANDREYEV: [*Perplexed*] Monday.

NATASHA: [*Going to the bed*] Wake up, Vanya, it's Monday.

IVAN: [*Behind curtain*] So what?

NATASHA: The doctor's come! [*Suddenly, the bed curtains swish back.*]

IVAN: Has he now? Well, isn't he the lucky one?

ANDREYEV: [*Terrified*] I say...what a remarkable bed!

NATASHA: It was a wedding gift.

IVAN: From the President.

ANDREYEV: Ah.

NATASHA: It belonged to the Bolkonsky family.

ANDREYEV: [*Drawn on*] Before the revolution.

IVAN: There weren't any Bolkonskys after the revolution.

ANDREYEV: [*Flustered*] Quite. [*He begins fishing in his bag.*]

41

IVAN: [*Deadpan*] It has its own pisspot.

ANDREYEV: You mean a commode.

IVAN: I mean a pisspot.... I empty it every day—out of the window of our seventeenth-floor luxury flat, overlooking the River Moscow.

NATASHA: Vanya, stop it.

IVAN: Comrade Prisipkin lives four floors down. I water his window-box—like a good peasant.

ANDREYEV: Shukhov, this isn't like you.

IVAN: I've changed: I'm the New Man. [*Whispering*] Can you keep a secret? Comrade Prisipkin has the best window-box in the world: it's fed on liquid sterabaloids.

ANDREYEV: [*Taken aback*] I don't know what you're talking about.

NATASHA: Neither do I. We never even use the pot.... It's full of dust.

IVAN: Like the Bolkonskys. [*NATASHA moves round the bed, pulls out a commode and holds up the large chamberpot.*]

NATASHA: Look.... That's funny. [*Slowly she turns the pot around, reading from it.*] 'Kilroy was here'....

IVAN: Bloody tourists! [*ANDREYEV takes the pot from NATASHA, and, anxious to change the tack, affects to examine it.*]

ANDREYEV: May I.... Ah, yes. Just needs a good clean.... Porcelain, I'd say.... Chinese. Second dynasty.... Fetch quite a bit, once upon a time.

IVAN: Not now, though.

ANDREYEV: [*Hurriedly*] Oh no, not now.

IVAN: Take it, then.

ANDREYEV: Me? What would I do with it?

IVAN: Piss in it.... We'll swap it for the good news you've brought.

ANDREYEV: [*Alarmed*] Good news?

IVAN: The results of the tests.... It is good news, isn't it? [*ANDREYEV is silent.*] Well, isn't it?

ANDREYEV: I'm afraid not.

IVAN: [*Scornful*] He's afraid not.

NATASHA: [*Frightened now*] Vanya!

IVAN: He's afraid he's gonna have to tell me I'm sterile, aren't you, doctor—pure dud sterile? Correction: he's worse than scared: he's wetting himself.

ANDREYEV: You can't imagine how upset I am.

IVAN: Should have used the pot!
    [*ANDREYEV puts the pot on the floor.*]

NATASHA: [*Shocked*] It's not true. It can't be true.

ANDREYEV: I'm afraid it is, my dear.

NATASHA: [*Despite herself*] But what about Mishkin's wife? She...

42

IVAN: What about Mishkin's wife? [*Pause*] Natasha—what about Mishkin's wife?

NATASHA: [*Eventually*] There was a child.

IVAN: You're lying.... [*NATASHA shakes her head.*] My child?

NATASHA: [*Nodding*] She had an abortion... Mishkin said it wasn't his. The Government didn't want any—trouble, during the Games... I swore I'd never tell you.

[*IVAN is shattered. He takes NATASHA in his arms.*]

IVAN: It wer' only a bit of fun....

ANDREYEV: I'd better go.

IVAN: You'd better not! You'd better tell me why I can give a child to a barren woman when I can't give one to my wife.

NATASHA: [*From IVAN's arms*] It's my fault!

IVAN: Come on, doctor. Be brave. Say it's not her fault at all. Tell her she's ripe for any man's kids- -'cept mine.... An' when you've finished, tell her I've got three sons already.

NATASHA: [*Crying out*] No!

IVAN: Tell her, doctor—three sons an' two daughters! Tell her how you put my seed in five other women- -an' now you've five brats I've never seen from five women I've never touched.

[*NATASHA is hysterical.*]

NATASHA: No! No!

IVAN: [*Relentless*] Then tell her she'll never have my child, however much I love her, 'cos there's only bad seed left in me.

NATASHA: [*Her head buried in IVAN's chest*] No!

IVAN: Then say I'm sorry. Don't forget that, doctor. Tell her I'm sorry. Say, Natalya, I'm sorry, I'm sorry.... [*He bows his head.*]

NATASHA: [*In a choking whisper*] I don't understand.

IVAN: [*Gazing straight at ANDREYEV*] Don't you? Don't you really? It's easy. Why've I had to give up lifting already? Why do my leg muscles tear, so that I can't walk for weeks on end? Why'm I a cripple? Why's my wife had to nurse me ever since we were wed? Why can't I even make love to her any more? Why? Why?

ANDREYEV: [*Seizing on a phrase*] What's that? Make love.... What's that?

IVAN: [*Shouting*] I can't make love to my wife, you little bastard! I'm a rotten gelding! [*NATASHA is moaning.*]

ANDREYEV: Are you sure?

IVAN: Am I sure? Sure I'm bloody sure!

ANDREYEV: [*Weakly, almost whispering*] I knew it.

IVAN: You all *knew* it. [*NATASHA raises her head.*] They knew those fuckin' drugs'd finish me! Drugs! They gave me drugs to make me grow—didn't you, doctor? To make me win. [*He draws NATASHA back to his chest, staring at ANDREYEV.*] An' what happens next, doctor? Does my hair fall out? Does

43

my heart collapse? Tell her what you've done, doctor!

ANDREYEV: [*Finally crying out*] They made me do it! [*IVAN is silent.*] Can you believe that? They made me—Kalogradov... and Prisipkin. We had orders from the President. You don't know, do you? It's the truth... [*Looking round him like a trapped animal.*] God, what if they're listening! No, no—why check on you? I told the coach: we don't know the side effects, I said; it could kill him, I said, for all we know—doses like that. He kept making me raise the dose, you see.... There was so little time—and you had to win, yes...the President said so.... And Prisipkin, he kept coming to scare me—kept bringing telegrams, kept telling me the Olympic Committee had found a trace for sterabaloids—they were going to ban them, he said, and we hadn't another drug ready, so we'd better push the dosage to the limit, while there was the chance. He was lying, of course. But it was too late then. Shukhov, I'm sorry...I have a wife and children. Every time I said 'no', they told me to remember Aksyonov. He'd've won the top lift at the last Olympics, they said, but his damnfool doctor got the dose wrong—too small—the dose was too small—and he lost. He was lucky, Aksyonov: it didn't do him much harm: he's an engineer up north now. But the doctor, nobody's seen him since. Just disappeared. They told me he was an orderly in a labour camp somewhere: he'd learned his lesson, they said—kept his prisoners working even when they were sick. Did I want to be a camp orderly? Did I want my wife sawing pine trees and my little girls freezing to death? Can you see, Shukhov? I'm only human. I wanted a laboratory—for my own research. When you'd won, they said, I could have any-thing—anything. Do you see how they do it? Then they said if anyone was to blame it was you. If you'd taken the drugs from the start, instead of being stupid—that's what they said —then the doses could have been lower. But you wasted so much time...that's what they said.... So I did as I was told. Is that so bad? My father, you know, he died—they killed him... he caught typhus in a camp before the war.... I have to be so careful. They're watching me all the time. I'm the President's personal physician—since the Games—and I'm still not safe.... [*IVAN stares at ANDREYEV. NATASHA has calmed now. Stung...*] I didn't have to come here. I could have sent some-one else.... Better look you over all the same? Don't you think? [*He fusses in his medical bag.*] Yes? Splendid. [*He steps across to the bed. NATASHA moves quietly aside. ANDREYEV lifts the back of IVAN's pyjamas. Using the stethoscope...*] Deep breaths now. Good.... Good.... Lie down, would you. [*IVAN lies full length, on the bed. His feet reach* over the end. *NATASHA, kneeling on the floor now, hugs them distractedly.*] Bodyweight back to normal, eh? Say 'ah'!

IVAN: [*As spatula is placed in his mouth*] Ah!

[*ANDREYEV speaks as he works, more confident now.*]

ANDREYEV: The muscle damage, it's permanent, I'm afraid. But the other things—the sterility—the, er, impotence...they may disappear with time, I just don't know. It's new ground.... Bowels all right, I presume. Yes.... No need to fret about your heart anyway. Sound as a bell. That's a blessing.... What will you do? Go home? Light job in the mines perhaps.... [*IVAN does not reply. The examination is over. IVAN sits up and fastens his pyjamas. NATASHA now sits beside him.*] By the way, I've brought your Army discharge papers. [*Fishing in his bag again, he hands over a form.*] There—you're a free man now.... Don't look at me like that, Shukhov. I can't stand it.... [*Pause. He picks up his bag.*] I'll make a full report, naturally. But it will have to be kept dark. If it got out that.... If you have any more bother, better ring me privately at the palace.... [*He makes to leave. IVAN and NATASHA watch him, silently.*]

IVAN: Aren't you forgettin' something?

ANDREYEV: What?

IVAN: [*Gently*] Your pisspot.

ANDREYEV: Oh yes. Thank you.... [*Picking it up.*] Thank you very much.... I'll let myself out.... Goodbye. [*He exits left, with pot and bag. IVAN and NATASHA sit in silence.*]

IVAN: [*Finally*] So it's true.

NATASHA: Oh Vanya, I've never heard such awful things. They must be monsters. How could they do that to you?

IVAN: Andreyev—is he a monster?

NATASHA: No, poor man—they forced him.

IVAN: Did they? Who forced him? The coach? Prisipkin? They're not monsters either—even Kalogradov. Who forced them? The Party? The President? Is the President a monster? We all did it, Natalya. Me too. I did it...I forgot who I was.

NATASHA: [*With great compassion*] You're not to blame.

IVAN: I wanted to be the strongest man in the world.

NATASHA: And you were: you won!

IVAN: I took their drugs.

NATASHA: What if you hadn't taken them?

IVAN: It was wrong!

NATASHA: It was for Russia!

IVAN: I'm ashamed for Russia!

NATASHA: [*Breaking away from him*] And who cares? In all Russia, who cares—except you and me? Russia doesn't even know why you've stopped lifting. It's all a big secret so no one finds out Russia cheated. Russia has crippled you! And we have to hide, half way up the sky, so the world won't guess the New Man can't have children! [*NATASHA is almost hysterical. IVAN slaps her face.*]

IVAN: Natasha!

NATASHA: [*Clinging back to him*] Vanya—what are we going to do? [*Pause*]

IVAN: [*Slowly, quietly*] We're going home.

NATASHA: To Sheremestvo?

IVAN: Like the doctor said.

NATASHA: [*Excited*] Oh yes, love, let's go home. Let's just be Shukhov and his wife—just two people. I'll be so proud.... Maybe you could find that lighter job. You'd soon be well, I know it. I could work at the hospital. Perhaps the house in the square will still be empty....

IVAN: [*Stopping her*] We're not running away. If we leave I've some things to do first.

NATASHA: Tell me.

IVAN: I've got to speak out against the drugs.

NATASHA: Yes, you must.

IVAN: I'll go to the Party, if I have to.

NATASHA: And then?

IVAN: I'm gonna smash this bloody bed!

NATASHA: [*Reckless, elated*] What about the President?

IVAN: Fuck the President!

NATASHA: [*Gleefully*] Not so loud.

IVAN: [*Whispering*] Fuck the President. [*He stands between the end-posts of the bed and stretches out his arms to grasp them. NATASHA watches, laughing.*]

NATASHA: You look like Samson! [*IVAN draws breath, and yanks the end-posts inward with a great shout.*]

IVAN: Brodsky! [*The bed collapses, IVAN with it.... Blackout.*]

SCENE TWO

Lights up. The gymnasium. On-screen, a large picture of IVAN, bar raised above his head in title-winning pose.... Music: the Red Army march tune. Enter, a vast weightlifter, DOBROVOLSKY, in red leotard, running at the double, in a circle, with coach KALOGRADOV behind him. While circling, knees up high, DOBROVOLSKY raises dumb-bells—left hand, right hand.

KALOGRADOV: Up, up, up, up, up.... Halt! At ease! [*He and DOBROVOLSKY stand together—DOBROVOLSKY holding the dumb-bells at his side.... Enter, SEMYONOV, very much the fussy television producer, puffing away on a bigger cigar. Also,* two TECHNICIANS, ANDREI and SASHA: one with hand-camera and tripod, the other with sound-boom and equipment.]

SEMYONOV: Ah, good day, colonel. Prompt as ever.... [KALO-GRADOV nods, curtly.] And this must be Corporal Dobro-volsky.... [DOBROVOLSKY grins, pleasantly.] What a story! Shukhov retires! The old champion face to face with his aspir-ing successor—the President's great discovery!

KALOGRADOV: [Cruelly] Corporal Dobrovolsky doesn't aspire, comrade: he just sweats. I'll tell you where the President dis-covered him—bending bars in the bleeding State circus.... [DOBROVOLSKY looks suitably ashamed.] Come on, you big ape, smile for the gentleman: he's going to make you famous.

SEMYONOV: Leave that to you, colonel. Just let me tell the tale. You know: the king is dead, long live the king—that sort of thing. [Enter IVAN, limping heavily.]

IVAN: 'Cept I'm not dead yet.

SEMYONOV: [Without a flicker] I should hope not, my dear Shukhov! [He leads IVAN to KALOGRADOV.] Did you know the coach has been promoted colonel?

IVAN: [Bitterly] What does he do to become a general?

SEMYONOV: And here is our new find, Corporal Dobrovolsky.... Corporal—meet Hero Shukhov.

IVAN: Hello.

DOBROVOLSKY: Hello. [DOBROVOLSKY smiles deferentially. IVAN gives him a bearhug of an embrace. The corporal res-ponds—drops one of the dumb-bells on KALOGRADOV's toe. He hops aside, howling with pain.]

KALOGRADOV: Aaah!

DOBROVOLSKY: Sorry, coach.

KALOGRADOV: I'll kill him! I'll bleeding murder him! [DOBROVOLSKY picks up the dumb-bell and resumes his position.]

SEMYONOV: Later, colonel, later.... Now, er, down to business. Ivan, you know the form, I think: we splash the announce-ment, quick spiel on the reasons, then a quick chat with the next champion.... OK?

IVAN: Yes.

SEMYONOV: Nervous?

IVAN: Bit.

SEMYONOV: [Grandly] Relax.... Everyone ready? Quiet please. Here we go.

ANDREI: Camera running.

SASHA: Sound on. [He raises the sound-boom above SEMYONOV and IVAN. KALOGRADOV and DOBROVOLSKY look on.]

SEMYONOV: [In his television voice] Hero Shukhov, Russia is

47

shocked to hear of your retirement from competitive sport. May I ask what prompted the decision?

IVAN: Yes...I'm a cripple.

SEMYONOV: [*Horrified*] Cut!

KALOGRADOV: Daft bugger! [*The TECHNICIANS adjust their equipment throughout this sequence.*]

SEMYONOV: Look, Vanya, love, you've got bad legs—all right, but does the whole world have to know? We'll try again. And let's have it straight this time: you're retiring undefeated—at your peak—OK? [*He signals to the TECHNICIANS.*]

ANDREI: Camera running.

SASHA: Sound on.

SEMYONOV: Comrade Shukhov, would you care to explain your shock retirement?

IVAN: [*Unabashed*] I wish to confess.

SEMYONOV: What?

IVAN: I took drugs.

SEMYONOV: Cut!... For Pete's sake!

KALOGRADOV: He's lying.

IVAN: It's the truth.

SEMYONOV: It's television!

IVAN: Can't I tell the truth on television?

SEMYONOV: You wanna get me shot?

IVAN: I'm not blaming anybody.

KALOGRADOV: [*Visibly bridling*] Whose fault is it, then, sunshine?

IVAN: Mine.

SEMYONOV: Yours? Ivan Shukhov's? You're blaming Ivan Shukhov?

IVAN: Yes.

SEMYONOV: You know who Ivan Shukhov is, don't you? He's a legend. People believe in him—millions of people. Are you gonna betray him because you've just dug up a conscience? Are you more important than Ivan Shukhov?

IVAN: I *am* Ivan Shukhov!

SEMYONOV: Then act like him! No more funny business, eh? This film's to be on the air by six.... Step up, corporal. [*He ushers DOBROVOLSKY across to the interview position, near IVAN—then signals to the TECHNICIANS.*]

ANDREI: Camera running.

SASHA: Sound on.

SEMYONOV: Hero Shukhov, have you any advice for Russia's new Olympic discovery?

IVAN: [*Looking straight at DOBROVOLSKY*] Don't let 'em give you any drugs.

SEMYONOV: [*Throwing up his hands in despair*] Cut!

48

IVAN: [*Regardless*] Especially not sterabaloids.
SEMYONOV: I said cut!
IVAN: Sterabaloids finished me.
SEMYONOV: [*Shrieking*] Cut!
IVAN: Made me impotent.
SEMYONOV: Cut! Cut! Cut! [*Now KALOGRADOV goes into action, facing IVAN, nose to nose.*]
KALOGRADOV: You're not just crippled, sunshine, you're bleeding crackers! [*Furiously, he advances on the poor TECHNICIANS.*] Show's over, boys. [*He seizes the camera and smashes it, ripping out the film.*]
SEMYONOV: [*Not very convincingly*] I'll want a receipt!
KALOGRADOV: Try this for size! [*He crushes the sound man's box equipment underfoot, twists the microphone boom into a circle and plonks it round SEMYONOV's neck, before grabbing him by the pants and hurling him off-stage.*]
SEMYONOV: [*Being ejected*] Aaah! [*The two TECHNICIANS gather their broken gear and escape.*]
KALOGRADOV: Bleeding fairies! [*Turning to IVAN.*] You too, sunshine. Clear off, before I rip your wings out.
IVAN: [*Unmoved*] I want to talk to the corporal.
KALOGRADOV: Well the corporal doesn't want to talk to you: the corporal hasn't heard a word you've said. [*DOBROVOL-SKY looks from IVAN to KALOGRADOV. Threateningly...*] Have you, corporal?
DOBROVOLSKY: No, coach.
KALOGRADOV: Don't let this creature kid you he's Shukhov. That's Ivan Shukhov, up there, [*Pointing to the screen picture.*] a giant, a patriot, a true Spartan. This thing, here, it's just a bag of pus. [*KALOGRADOV kicks IVAN behind the knees. IVAN falls to the ground, crying out with pain.*] What did I tell you? He's an old man already: his muscles tear like bleeding petals.... Come on, sunshine, who's gonna stuff your country bitch now? [*IVAN struggles to his feet. KALOGRAD-OV moves back alongside DOBROVOLSKY.*] Drugs made him impotent, he says. Hah bloody hah! He hadn't the spunk of a sick spider to start with. [*IVAN, arms outstretched, pleads to DOBROVOLSKY.*]
IVAN: Don't listen!
KALOGRADOV: [*Merciless*] Those five brats he spawned—mewling little runts, every one: they're still in bleeding incubators.
IVAN: Don't believe him!
KALOGRADOV: They want putting down, like their lousy father.
IVAN: [*A bellow of pain and anger*] Bastard! [*DOBROVOLSKY drops his dumb-bells again, one on KALOGRADOV's foot —the same foot.*]

KALOGRADOV: [*Hopping away*] Aaah! Whaddya do that for?

DOBROVOLSKY: You said to put them down, coach.

KALOGRADOV: Not the dumb-bells, baboon—you've broken my bleeding toe. [*He sits down and examines his foot.*]

DOBROVOLSKY: [*Sympathetically to IVAN*] I'm sorry.... You should go now.

IVAN: I came to warn you.

KALOGRADOV: [*Massaging his toe*] Get that filth out of here, corporal.

DOBROVOLSKY: Yes, coach.

IVAN: [*Urgently*] The Games—they're a sham: you'll never win without drugs!

DOBROVOLSKY: [*Simply*] I'll take my chance.

IVAN: No!

DOBROVOLSKY: You took yours.

IVAN: I didn't know what would happen to me! [*KALOGRADOV is back on his feet now, training shoe in hand.*]

KALOGRADOV: He's jealous: he wants to stop you beating his record.

IVAN: [*Taking off his jacket*] You'll have to choose, corporal; I'm not leaving. [*DOBROVOLSKY looks from one to the other.*]

KALOGRADOV: [*Advancing with a hop*] Either you bleeding shift him or I'll have you back feeding camels. What's it to be? [*Reluctantly, DOBROVOLSKY moves towards IVAN. They both circle for position; IVAN reaches out his right arm: DOBROVOLSKY takes it.*]

IVAN: You're destroying yourself!

KALOGRADOV: Go for his legs, you fool! Go for his legs! [*DOBROVOLSKY spins IVAN round and grabs one of his ankles. IVAN falls forward. As he lies, DOBROVOLSKY forces the leg up his back. Once more, IVAN yells in agony. KALOGRADOV, ecstatic, bends like a wrestling referee and slaps the floor with his shoe.*] One! Two! Three! Out! [*DOBROVOLSKY looks down upon his victim, picks up his dumb-bells and exits. KALOGRADOV gloats...*] This is the Palace of Physical Culture, sunshine: 'mens sana in corpore sano'.... Next time, he'll bust every bone in your bleeding body! [*He hops off-stage, after DOBROVOLSKY, shouting.*] Oi, Tarzan, come and lick my toe! [*As KALOGRADOV exits, the stage lights go down, leaving a spotlight on IVAN, as he struggles to his knees, gazing silently at the audience. Cut screen-picture.*]

SCENE THREE

Across the darkened stage—behind IVAN, kneeling in the spot-light—are placed three file-stacked desks, with high seats. At stage left, a column-base, containing flowers. Over the desks, a sign: DEPARTMENT OF PLEAS, PROTESTS AND PETITIONS. Lights up, on the left-hand desk, where there sits an OFFICIAL, checking papers. On the screen, a picture of a long corridor, with dozens of rooms leading off.... Slowly, IVAN rises, looks round, then approaches the FIRST OFFICIAL, limping badly. The FIRST OFFICIAL ignores him. IVAN clears his throat. The FIRST OFFICIAL seems oblivious.

IVAN: [*Finally*] 'Scuse me.

FIRST OFFICIAL: [*Reaching for a form, without looking up*] Name?

IVAN: Shukhov.

FIRST OFFICIAL: In full.

IVAN: Shukhov—Ivan Denisovich.

FIRST OFFICIAL: [*Writing*] Shukhov? Funny, that's the tenth Shukhov in two days. My father used to get Romanovs: I get Shukhovs. [*IVAN waits. Brusque again...*] Business?

IVAN: I'd like to see Comrade Prisipkin.

FIRST OFFICIAL: Which Comrade Prisipkin?

IVAN: A.L. Prisipkin.

FIRST OFFICIAL: Mines.

IVAN: No, Sport.

FIRST OFFICIAL: [*Insistent*] Mines! He's been promoted. Minister of Mines.

IVAN: Can I see him?

FIRST OFFICIAL: [*Without looking up, spiking the form*] He's busy.

IVAN: Can I wait?

FIRST OFFICIAL: There's a queue.

IVAN: What about tomorrow?

FIRST OFFICIAL: There'll still be a queue.... There's always a queue. [*IVAN waits. The FIRST OFFICIAL continues working.*] Good day.

IVAN: [*Hesitant*] Er....

FIRST OFFICIAL: [*Sighing*] What now?

IVAN: Is Professor Abuladze about?

FIRST OFFICIAL: [*Reaching for another form*] Department?

IVAN: [*Doubtfully*] People's Anatomy.

FIRST OFFICIAL: Promoted...Minister of Health.

IVAN: Can I see him?

FIRST OFFICIAL: [*Spiking the form*] He's sick. [*Pause*]

IVAN: [*Without much hope*] General Velikovsky?

FIRST OFFICIAL: [*Sternly*] Field Marshal.

IVAN: Sorry.... Is he—?

FIRST OFFICIAL: Restored to active service—Eastern front.

IVAN: Oh. [*Disappointed, he turns away. The FIRST OFFICIAL puts down his pen.*]

FIRST OFFICIAL: You could try the President.... [*IVAN turns back.*] They all try the President in the end.

IVAN: [*Encouraged*] The President....

FIRST OFFICIAL: Second on the left, down the corridor, first flight of stairs and through the swing door, next to the statue.

IVAN: Thanks. [*He limps up-stage, towards the screen.*]

FIRST OFFICIAL: [*Watching him*] There's a lift if you....
[*The FIRST OFFICIAL shrugs and resumes his work. Momentary blackout. Lights up, then, on the centre desk. IVAN is waiting beside it. Seated, at work, is SECOND OFFICIAL.*]

IVAN: 'Scuse me.

SECOND OFFICIAL: Name?

IVAN: Shukhov.

SECOND OFFICIAL: In full.

IVAN: Shukhov—Ivan Denisovich.

SECOND OFFICIAL: Business?

IVAN: I wondered...

SECOND OFFICIAL: Spit it out, man.

IVAN: I want to see the President.

SECOND OFFICIAL: Have you filled in a form?

IVAN: [*Plucking up courage*] Now.

SECOND OFFICIAL: Impossible.

IVAN: Why?

SECOND OFFICIAL: He's busy.

IVAN: It's a matter of life an' death.

SECOND OFFICIAL: It always is.

IVAN: [*Less overawed now*] I'm serious.

SECOND OFFICIAL: [*Glancing up for the first time*] Look, there's a queue for 'life and death matters': some people have been in it for years—and no one's died yet.

IVAN: [*Shocked*] Can't the President see them?

SECOND OFFICIAL: The President sees 'matters of life and death' before leaving for the weekend. [*Peering at IVAN.*] Today's Tuesday—and you are the last in the queue.... Of course, there may be ways and means of, shall we say, expediting the affair.

IVAN: Those people in the queue, who expedites their affairs?

SECOND OFFICIAL: [*Matter of fact*] I do—if they pay.

IVAN: An' what if they don't?

SECOND OFFICIAL: It can hardly be a matter of life and death, can it? [*He returns to his work.*]

52

IVAN: [*At last*] How much? [*The SECOND OFFICIAL looks up.
  Testily...*] How much do you want?
SECOND OFFICIAL: [*Casually*] Oh...fifty?
IVAN: Kopecks?
SECOND OFFICIAL: Roubles.
IVAN: Ballocks.
SECOND OFFICIAL: As you wish.
IVAN: [*Feeling in his pocket*] There's three. I've no more on me.
SECOND OFFICIAL: [*Head down*] Borrow some.
IVAN: Where from?
SECOND OFFICIAL: We have excellent credit facilities--across
  the corridor, up two flights, green door on your left. [*Momen-
  tary blackout. Lights up, on the right-hand desk. IVAN stands,
  waiting. Seated, at work, THIRD OFFICIAL.*]
THIRD OFFICIAL: Amount?
IVAN: [*Surprised*] Er—forty-seven roubles. [*The THIRD OFFIC-
  IAL counts the notes out on to his desk, then sits waiting.
  IVAN eventually decides he must be meant to take them.*]
THIRD OFFICIAL: Not so fast. Name?
IVAN: Shukhov—Ivan Denisovich.
THIRD OFFICIAL: Address?
IVAN: Flat 600, House of the Champions.
THIRD OFFICIAL: Job?
IVAN: Miner.
THIRD OFFICIAL: Application refused! There are no miners in
  Champion House. [*The THIRD OFFICIAL sweeps the notes
  back off the table.*]
IVAN: Weightlifter! [*The THIRD OFFICIAL roars with laughter.*]
  Retired. [*Another burst of laughter. IVAN produces a card.*]
  Look! Ivan Shukhov! Hero of all the Russias!
THIRD OFFICIAL: [*Viciously*] 'Obble off, 'Ercules, 'fore I 'ave
  yer locked up. [*Momentary blackout. Light, now, on all three
  desks: all THREE OFFICIALS busy with their papers. IVAN
  is waiting again, at the middle desk.*]
IVAN: Application refused....
SECOND OFFICIAL: Hard cheese, old chap.
IVAN: It's no joke: I'm trying to save a man's life.
SECOND OFFICIAL: You need a doctor.
IVAN: Doctor Andreyev!
SECOND OFFICIAL: What about him?
IVAN: He could vouch for me.
SECOND OFFICIAL: Doctor Andreyev's engaged- -with the Pres-
  ident. [*The FIRST and THIRD OFFICIALS exchange know-
  ing grins.*]
IVAN: Just tell him I'm here. He'll see me. Just tell him who I am!
SECOND OFFICIAL: And who, precisely, are you?

53

IVAN: The strongest man in the world!

SECOND OFFICIAL: [*Laughing, spitefully*] Sit down a second: I'll send for an ambulance. [*His mocking laughter is taken up by the other OFFICIALS.*]

IVAN: [*Backing away, very agitated*] Why won't you listen? Why won't you help me? Why do you pretend you're all the same? [*Another wave of laughter.*] Stop laughing at me! D'you hear? Stop pretending. Listen to me. I must see the President. [*Laughter*] I've got a complaint. [*Laughter*] I've got rights. [*Laughter*] I wish to protest. [*Laughter*] I protest! [*Yelling*] I protest! [*All at once, the laughter has stopped: IVAN's final cry is completely exposed.*]

SECOND OFFICIAL: Do you now?

IVAN: [*Defiant*] Yes.

SECOND OFFICIAL: Are you quite sure?

IVAN: Yes.

FIRST OFFICIAL, SECOND OFFICIAL, THIRD OFFICIAL: [*Speaking in turn*] Protests down five flights./Lift available. /Take the red door on the right and walk straight on./Can't miss it. [*The OFFICIALS exit; IVAN moves aside, in despair. Enter, a FOURTH OFFICIAL, an attractive woman.*]

FOURTH OFFICIAL: Name?

IVAN: [*Startled*] Shukhov.... Ivan Denisovich.

FOURTH OFFICIAL: You wish to protest about the treatment of Soviet athletes.

IVAN: Yes.

FOURTH OFFICIAL: Very well: it's time we had a chat. While you're here we can discuss your impersonation of the hero Shukhov.

IVAN: Go to blazes!

FOURTH OFFICIAL: Behave yourself.

IVAN: I'll show you who I am! [*IVAN seizes the column-base and hoists it into the air. Beneath it is a POLICEMAN, in black uniform.*]

FOURTH OFFICIAL: Arrest that man!

IVAN: What for? [*The POLICEMAN confronts IVAN, who backs away, armed with the base.*]

FOURTH OFFICIAL: Arrest that man! [*From the desk-fronts, more POLICEMEN appear, surrounding IVAN.*]

IVAN: I haven't done anything. [*Bewildered, he puts down the base and is hustled off-stage.... Blackout.*]

SCENE FOUR

Around the stage, an up-ended trunk, suitcases, furniture covered in white sheets. As the lights rise, NATASHA is sitting tensely, in an armchair, a telephone on her knee. On-screen, the Moscow skyline.

NATASHA: Ring. Please, please ring.... Ohhh! [*She bangs the telephone down on top of the trunk. Pause. She picks up the receiver.*] Operator. Operator. Hallo, hallo. Operator... [*With no reply she seems to give up.*] What's going on? Vanya, where are you? [*Desperately*] Operator, can you hear me? Can anybody hear me? [*There is no reply, but NATASHA continues.*] Where's my husband? There's something wrong, isn't there? We should have been on the train now... [*Sudden presentiment.*] He's in trouble, isn't he? Operator. Operator. Please listen. [*Crying out.*] Somebody listen!
[*Enter IVAN—still limping badly.*] Vanya! Oh, Vanya love, you're safe! [*She runs to him, throws her arms around him.*]

IVAN: Natasha!

NATASHA: I was so scared.

IVAN: So was I.

NATASHA: You look like a ghost! Come and sit down. [*She takes IVAN to the armchair.*] I've got everything packed, see— [*IVAN sits, head in hands. Alarmed...*] Vanya—whatever's happened? Where've you been? [*Helplessly*] We've missed the train!

IVAN: [*At last*] They arrested me.

NATASHA: [*Incredulous*] What?

IVAN: Said I was acting suspicious...

NATASHA: Who?

IVAN: ...disgracing myself.

NATASHA: Who did? Who arrested you?

IVAN: Secret police.

NATASHA: Never! Not you! They couldn't have!

IVAN: Kept questioning me, different people—over and over —shining lights in my eyes.... They wouldn't let me sleep. Made me stand up—kept making me stand up.... My legs. My bloody legs!

NATASHA: Oh, Vanya...

IVAN: In the end they brought Andreyev.

NATASHA: Andreyev! [*She springs up.*] I knew we shouldn't have given him that pisspot!

IVAN: No, no. I asked for him. I thought he could explain.... They fetched him, at two in the morning, poor sod, in his dressing-gown—petrified.... He told 'em I was sick. So they let me go—in a taxi—they found me a taxi.... Said it was a

55

warning: get back to Sheremestvo an' keep my mouth shut
—or they'd shut it for me.

NATASHA: [*Momentarily defiant*] They're not allowed! Not any
more.... Are they? [*IVAN is silent.*] That explains the phone....
[*IVAN doesn't understand.*] It's out of order.... I couldn't get
through to anyone. [*All at once, the telephone—on the suit-
case—begins to ring.*] Vanya, I swear... [*IVAN picks up the
receiver.*]

IVAN: [*Doubtfully*] Hello.... Yes.... Oh.... Thank you.... [*Replacing the receiver.*] It was the operator: she's reconnected us:
we were accidentally cut off.

NATASHA: For two days!... [*Shiver of fear.*] Vanya, we're going
to do as they say, aren't we? We're going home.... When's the
next train? [*The telephone rings. Again IVAN answers.*]

IVAN: Hello.... Thank you. [*He puts back the receiver. Express-
ionless...*] Midnight.

NATASHA: What?

IVAN: The next train to Sheremestvo...

NATASHA: How did they...?

IVAN: How the hell do I know? [*Silence. The phone rings again.*]

NATASHA: Don't answer it. [*Incensed, IVAN seizes the receiver
and yells into it.*]

IVAN: What the blazes is going on? [*Taken aback by the reply, he
listens for a moment then shouts again.*] Get stuffed!... I said:
get stuffed! It's not for sale! [*IVAN replaces the receiver. As
calmly as he can*] Carpenter—called Dimshits—with a brother
in the police department.... He wanted to buy our black-
market wood.

NATASHA: [*Baffled*] We haven't got any black-market wood.

IVAN: He meant the bed.

NATASHA: [*Astounded*] You told the police about the bed?

IVAN: I had to tell 'em something.

NATASHA: [*Horror-struck*] Why?

IVAN: They knew I'd borrowed the axe...Natalya, they know
everything. I said I'd chopped up the bed for firewood.

NATASHA: But we've got central heating!

IVAN: Who cares? Who bloody cares? [*Angrily, IVAN yanks out
the telephone wire.*]

NATASHA: Now look what you've done! [*From off-stage, loud
knocking.*] What if it's the police? [*Again, knocking.*] Hide
it somewhere! [*Looking around, IVAN pulls off one of the
dustsheets.... Beneath it is revealed a man sitting, stone-
faced in a second armchair. NATASHA jumps to IVAN's
side. Aghast, they watch as the man rises.*]

POLICE SPY: That's an offence, that is.

IVAN: [*Holding sheet and telephone*] What?

POLICE SPY: Tampering with a Party line.... Do you mind? [*He takes the telephone from IVAN and winds in the loose wire. With a click of the heels, he bows and turns to leave. IVAN screws up the sheet and hurls it at the POLICE SPY's back.*]

IVAN: Bugger off! [*The POLICE SPY stops, swings round, looks at the sheet at his feet, then at IVAN.*]

POLICE SPY: You've not heard the last of this. [*He exits, tipping his hat to SEMYONOV, who passes him entering.*]

SEMYONOV: Did you get his name?

IVAN: Kilroy!

NATASHA: [*Almost beside herself*] I fell asleep, Vanya—but I never left the flat.... Believe me.

SEMYONOV: Don't panic.... Have a drink. [*SEMYONOV takes a half-empty bottle of vodka from his pocket and hands it to IVAN, who slumps into one of the armchairs and takes a swig. NATASHA, nervously, peeps under the remaining sheets.*]

NATASHA: He couldn't have been there all the time....

SEMYONOV: Lady, they've got the place staked out: there's one in the caretaker's room and another in the doorway over the street.

NATASHA: [*Scornful*] How did you fly in, then?

SEMYONOV: Press! I've brought your wedding photographs...as a going-away present. [*He fishes an album out of his inside pocket.*]

IVAN: We're not going away.

NATASHA: [*Seizing the bottle*] Oh hell, he'll be drunk!

IVAN: [*Seizing it back*] Have a heart. [*He takes another enormous swig. SEMYONOV stretches out on the sheet-covered sofa, lighting a cigar.*]

NATASHA: [*To SEMYONOV*] It's your fault. Giving him vodka. He hasn't slept for two days.

IVAN: [*Soberly*] I said we're not going away.

NATASHA: Vanya, love, stop babbling. We've got to go—back to Sheremestvo.

IVAN: [*With casual finality*] I've changed my mind. [*Again he drinks. Meanwhile, SEMYONOV is casually leafing through the photograph album.*]

NATASHA: [*Excitedly*] We can't stay here. I hate it! This flat —I hate it! Moscow—all those people—what are they doing? Nobody needs us, nobody wants us any more—not since you've been ill. We never see anyone—not their faces anyway, only their backs, Vanya, never their eyes.... And it's always so cold.... The sun's gone grey.... [*She shivers.*] I'm so unhappy, Vanya. Please—let's go home!

IVAN: [*Gazing sadly at the bottle*] Home? [*Slowly he tips up the*

bottle. It is empty.... NATASHA seizes the album from
SEMYONOV and sits by IVAN, on the chair arm, showing
him the photographs. At each turn of the page, the appro-
priate scene appears on the screen.]

NATASHA: Look, love—look at these pictures.... That's where we
belong. [*On-screen, a shot of an industrial-farming community,*
seen from the forested hillsides around it. Then, as NATASHA
turns the pages, the pithead gear; fields and orchards, bordering
a river.]

SEMYONOV: [*Sardonic*] Ah, Sheremestvo! The real Russia!

NATASHA: How would you know? [*Again she turns the page.*
Now, on-screen, we see IVAN's mining friends, holding out
drinking glasses to the camera.] Those faces, Vanya—couldn't
you just kiss them? Alexei, Nikolai...our people! [*Another*
page: this time, a happy wedding group, all in best gear,
country style. In the background, quite small, three crows....]
Ooops! [*She laughs again.*] That's when you tripped on the
red carpet.... Remember? [*On the new page, we see IVAN,*
on his backside, while NATASHA tries to help him up. Once
more, not particularly conspicuous, the three crows....] Here
you are again—playing the balalaika...Vanya, how long is it
since you played the balalaika? [*Now the screen-picture is of*
IVAN, in shirt sleeves and knee-length boots, playing the bala-
laika, while dancing on a trestle table.... The next pages show
a dance and Alexei and friends, playing fiddles, etc.] And the
dancing! Oh Vanya, the dancing! My head whirled, I thought
the earth had spun loose in the sky.... Vanya, let's go back.
[*Gently, IVAN takes the book from her, closes it, draws her*
down on to her knees in front of him and holds her face in his
hands.]

IVAN: Natasha.... There's no going back—not now...not yet.

NATASHA: [*Turning her head*] Something terrible's happening.
I can feel it. [*Pause. On-screen again, the Moscow skyline.*]

SEMYONOV: [*Taunting*] Maybe she's right, Shukhov. Take that
old midnight train: mosey home through the birch forests and
let Russia forget you.
[*IVAN takes the bait, springing from the chair in a fury of*
drink and emotion.]

IVAN: Forget me? You little ponce! Russia doesn't even *know* me
any more. All Russia knows is that bloody monument in the
Hall of Heroes. People pay to walk past it: thousands of 'em.
They get bits of paper given and they're supposed to say the
words: 'Hail Ivan Shukhov, son of Russia!' It's written on the
paper for 'em. 'To this may all Russians aspire'! I ask you. It's
twelve foot tall, that bloody monument! An' there's me limping round, listening, and no cunt recognizes me. I feel like

telling 'em—yelling it out—'It's a lie, a bloody lie! That's not
Ivan Shukhov! I'm Ivan Shukhov! I'm the New Man! An' look
what it's done to me!' [*SEMYONOV gets up and approaches
IVAN, puffing his cigar.*]

SEMYONOV: Now that's more like it.

NATASHA: Vulture!

SEMYONOV: Lady, I want to help.... On the level.

NATASHA: Don't trust him, Vanya.

SEMYONOV: [*Taking out a letter*] Just read this letter.... I've got
contacts, Shukhov. Give me two hours and I'll have you on
every front page from Washington to Wogga-Wogga.
[*NATASHA snatches the letter.*]

IVAN: What does it say?

SEMYONOV: It's your confession: your appeal to the world.

NATASHA: [*Reading*] 'Destroyed by drugs! Sick Soviet strong-
man tells all!' [*IVAN takes the letter.*]

IVAN: Ballocks!

SEMYONOV: [*Carried away*] 'Ivan Shukhov, the strongest man in
the world, lies under house arrest in Moscow today, awaiting
the train that will carry him to exile!'

NATASHA: It's a lie!

SEMYONOV: It's your only hope.

IVAN: Turning traitor? [*He pockets the letter.*]

SEMYONOV: Rather be a martyr, would you? Dying for the
cause and all that crap? Because believe me, they'll be wheel-
ing your coffin out right now.

IVAN: If there's one to fit me.

SEMYONOV: No problem: they'll chop your feet off and post
'em home with a note from Army surplus.

NATASHA: [*Horrified*] Stop it!

SEMYONOV: Look, you wanted to protest, didn't you? In Russia,
protesting's like peeing into the wind. But protesting to the
enemy, now that's different. With a posse of foreign pressmen
on your doorstep, the worst they can do is expel you.

IVAN: [*Incredulous*] Expel me?

SEMYONOV: To America.... You'd get a ticker-tape reception.

IVAN: I hate America!

SEMYONOV: Better bled than dead, though, eh? Anyway, Natasha could probably join you.

NATASHA: No!

IVAN: I can't do it!

SEMYONOV: That's the booze talking.

IVAN: [*Impassioned*] Wrong! It's me—Ivan Shukhov—the one and
only—accept no bloody substitute! Let me tell you something,
dungman... [*He rampages round the room.*] an' if there's any
more woodworm in here, you can listen, too...I love Russia!

Do you hear that, you lick-spittlers? Three cheers for the fucking revolution! Don't ask me to betray my country, Semyonov. Russia's mine! The revolution's mine—my family died for it, like millions of others.... That's what I believe....

SEMYONOV: [*Changing tack*] OK, OK, I give in.... So what's your plan, Superman?

IVAN: [*Decidedly*] I'm gonna bust that flaming monument!

SEMYONOV: Come again.

IVAN: The monument—I'm going to smash it.

SEMYONOV: The Shukhov monument?

IVAN: Yes.

SEMYONOV: Christ!

NATASHA: [*Breathless*] Vanya!

SEMYONOV: When?

IVAN: Tonight.

SEMYONOV: Er, need any help?

IVAN: [*Smiling*] You know there'll be trouble.

SEMYONOV: Isn't that the big idea?

NATASHA: [*Frightened*] Vanya, what does he mean?

IVAN: This time, I'm gonna give 'em something to try me for, then I can defend myself—I can testify in court about the drugs, about Dobrovolsky.... Don't worry, Natalya—the law'll protect me.

NATASHA: [*Suddenly, eyes ablaze*] Yes, Vanya, go to the law!

SEMYONOV: We'll have to get out of the flat first: we're surrounded.

IVAN: [*Sarcastic*] Use your pass. I'll slip down the incinerator chute.

SEMYONOV: Sometimes, it all seems worthwhile!

IVAN: Meet me by the river.

SEMYONOV: You bet. [*SEMYONOV exits, hurriedly. NATASHA runs to IVAN's side.*]

NATASHA: [*Agitated*] What about me? Don't leave me here!

IVAN: [*Forceful*] I'll need someone to speak for me in court.

NATASHA: No... [*She rushes for her coat.*]

IVAN: [*Stopping her*] Natasha! Keep the door locked. Semyonov'll pass you a message about the trial.... [*Tenderly now.*] Goodbye! [*He draws her to him and kisses her.*] If things go wrong, make for Sheremestvo.

NATASHA: [*As he exits*] Not without you.... Never, without you! [*Stage lights fade to darkness, as NATASHA sits, disconsolately, on one of the suitcases. Silence. On-screen, the wedding group, from the photograph album, with the three crows in the background. In a series of shots, the crows are gradually enlarged, until they alone fill the whole screen. For a moment, this picture is held—then cut.*]

SCENE FIVE

Heroic music. Down-stage, right, an enormous model of IVAN, in the heroic Socialist Realist style, showing him, naked, straining to hold a vast weight above his head. The model, almost twice life-size, stands on a plinth (it is made, possibly, of painted muslin, like a 'sculpted' air balloon, inflated to a smooth tension). Beside it, a signboard, with the legend: THE STRONGEST MAN IN THE WORLD.... To the left, and a little up-stage, a second, smaller model, complete with military cap, moustache and greatcoat, pinned to which is a big card: COMRADE STALIN. Left again, and further up-stage, a still smaller model, of COMRADE LENIN, with the appropriate card. Finally, completing the perspective, an empty plinth, up-stage left.... Down-stage, left, a large chair; also a table, with bellpush and 'Alarm' sign. Suspended across the stage, a red banner, announcing: HALL OF SOVIET HEROES.... Cut music. Silence. Low light picks out the statues. Now, a creaking noise, front-stage, as a trapdoor is slowly raised. SEMYONOV emerges, wearing a frock-coat. Behind him, IVAN, in his miner's helmet.

IVAN: Gimme a hand with this gear. [*IVAN passes out a pick-axe and a small holdall, with the initials CCCP—then climbs out of the trap.*]

SEMYONOV: I tell you: the pickaxe is beyond me.... That monument– it's plastic: they're all plastic.

IVAN: I know.

SEMYONOV: So, Soviet heroes change too fast for stone. So, you don't need a pickaxe: you need a pin.

IVAN: [*Firmly*] I need a pickaxe. [*IVAN is checking the contents of the holdall: track-suit, documents and a medal, which he kisses.*]

SEMYONOV: [*Musing*] Wonder how moles do it?

IVAN: What?

SEMYONOV: See in the dark.

IVAN: [*Laughing*] They've got red noses. [*IVAN peers round at the statues, using the light on his helmet. SEMYONOV puts on a white wig and beard.*]

SEMYONOV: [*Meanwhile*] Before the revolution, you know, the Czar's gardeners used to ambush moles in his ornamental shrubbery. Every time they shot one, another began tunnelling. First, they ruined the lawns, then they toppled the statues, then one day the Czar fell down a well and was never seen again.

IVAN: And then?

SEMYONOV: The moles moved into the Kremlin. 'Right,' they said, 'no more tunnels.' And we all live happily ever after....

[Suddenly, the stage lights click full on. IVAN and SEMYO-NOV stand, rooted to the spot. At stage left, the hall CARE-TAKER, a fat, old woman in balaclava, apron and wellington boots, carrying an ancient blunderbuss.]

CARETAKER: Blimey, Moscow underground!
   [SEMYONOV keeps his back to the CARETAKER; IVAN now moves cautiously towards her.]

IVAN: You wouldn't turn us in!

CARETAKER: Bet your sweet fanny.... I've only to press this bell.... *[Levelling the gun at him, as he comes nearer.]*

IVAN: Don't you know me?

CARETAKER: Jews, are yer? Intillectuals? Anarchists?

IVAN: *[Limping nearer still]* Look closer.

CARETAKER: Keep back!

IVAN: I won't hurt you.
   [Driven backwards, the CARETAKER trips and falls on to her chair; the seat gives way beneath her.]

CARETAKER: Aaagh! *[She is stuck, her bloomered rump below the chair bottom. As she collapses, the gun accidentally fires upwards. SEMYONOV rushes to hide behind a plinth; IVAN drops flat on his face. From the flies, falls a large, dead crow. IVAN gets to his knees, looks fearfully around. Nothing happens.]*

SEMYONOV: *[Round the corner of the plinth]* What is it?

IVAN: *[Baffled]* A crow.

CARETAKER: *[Excitedly]* Crow? Crow, did you say? *[IVAN picks up the bird. Triumphantly...]* Got 'im! Mucky little 'orror! Bin soilin' mi statues! *[IVAN takes the gun and puts it, with the crow, on the table.]*

IVAN: Put him in a pie, comrade. *[SEMYONOV, creeping up on the CARETAKER, pulls her balaclava round, back to front, then holds her from behind, as she struggles.]*

SEMYONOV: Quick—get on with it.

CARETAKER: *[Muffled]* Rape! Murder! *[IVAN rushes across stage, spits on his hands and swings back the pick....]*

IVAN: *[Crying out]* Down with the Hero Shukhov!

SEMYONOV: Down with the cult of personality!

CARETAKER: *[As SEMYONOV holds her]* Madmen! Lunatics! *[Loudly, the Soviet national anthem rings out. IVAN summons himself and, with a mighty shout, strikes a blow with the pickaxe at the groin of his own image.]*

IVAN: Brodsky! *[Standing back, he salutes. Slowly, the model deflates. As it finally flops, the anthem cuts.]*

SEMYONOV: Bit low, weren't you—bit below the belt?

IVAN: Couldn't reach any higher.

CARETAKER: Sabotage!

SEMYONOV: Feel better?

IVAN: [*Exalted*] I feel free!

SEMYONOV: Exit the dungman. [*He lets go of the yelling CARE-TAKER, climbs on to the empty plinth, hangs a white card, saying KARL MARX, around his neck, and settles into a statuesque pose, right arm raised from the elbow.*]

CARETAKER: Help! Help! [*IVAN leans the pick against the plinth and lifts the CARETAKER out of the chair. As he pulls her balaclava back round she sees the fallen statue.*] Oh, you 'aven't! You couldn't 'ave! Wha'd'ya do a thing like that for?

IVAN: Never mind, old lady—just ring the bell.

CARETAKER: 'Ere, where's your friend?

IVAN: Flown. [*She looks at him, shrugging.*]

CARETAKER: S'your funeral. If I don't ring them, they'll ring me—wring mi bloody neck! [*The CARETAKER presses the alarm. Buzzers sound. From a hidden door in the plinth of the Stalin statue, five POLICEMEN in uniform pour out and surround IVAN, with drawn batons. Following them, the female FOURTH OFFICIAL, relaxed, smoking.*]

FOURTH OFFICIAL: Stay exactly where you are. Do exactly as I say. Janitress grade two, Sokolska, your report.

CARETAKER: [*Grabbing her gun*] Caught 'im red-handed, slashin' Shukhov's monument.

FOURTH OFFICIAL: So we meet again, Hero Shukhov.

CARETAKER: Shukhov? Never!

FOURTH OFFICIAL: Silence! [*The CARETAKER shrivels.*] Evidently, comrade, you wish to destroy yourself: we shall render every assistance.... Arrest that man! [*Before the POLICEMEN can move, IVAN intervenes.*]

IVAN: I surrender.

FOURTH OFFICIAL: A technicality.

IVAN: [*Pointing to the plinth*] I also hand over certain effects.

FOURTH OFFICIAL: As you wish.... Sergeant, make an inventory. [*The FIRST POLICEMAN takes out notebook and pencil; the SECOND POLICEMAN checks the contents of the bag, etc.*]

SECOND POLICEMAN: One pickaxe; one track-suit; one medal, gold; one priority shopping card; keys and permit; pension book; disability certificate...

FOURTH OFFICIAL: Aren't you forgetting something?

IVAN: [*Hesitantly*] No...

FOURTH OFFICIAL: Your Party card.

IVAN: I want to keep it.

FOURTH OFFICIAL: Criminals cannot be Party members...and vice versa.

63

IVAN: [*Impassioned*] I'm not a criminal: I've not been tried.
FOURTH OFFICIAL: Seize him! [*The POLICEMEN hesitate.*]
IVAN: I am a loyal citizen of the Soviet Union.
FOURTH OFFICIAL: I said seize him! [*Now the POLICEMEN
    attack, raining baton blows upon IVAN's head. But IVAN
    still wears the miner's helmet.*] Fools, fools! Take his helmet
    off! [*IVAN struggles but is finally held, the helmet is pulled
    off and he is batoned to his knees.*] The card! The card!
    [*IVAN's head is held back by the hair: a POLICEMAN
    searches his pockets.*]
THIRD POLICEMEN: Here, comrade.
FOURTH OFFICIAL: Identity papers!
IVAN: [*Struggling again*] No!
FOURTH OFFICIAL: In Russia, the criminal forfeits his identity.
    [*The POLICEMAN hands over the cards, the FOURTH
    OFFICIAL rips them to pieces. IVAN collapses.*] Immobilize
    him.
THIRD POLICEMAN: [*With another find*] There's a letter, too.
FOURTH OFFICIAL: File it. [*Ropes are produced. IVAN is
    thrown on to his back, his hands and feet are tied, batons are
    inserted through the ropes and he is carted off-stage like a
    dead animal. The CARETAKER spits on him as he passes.
    The POLICEMEN take the pickaxe and effects, as evidence.*]
CARETAKER: Swine! He tried to shoot me!
FOURTH OFFICIAL: Return to your duties, Janitress Sokolska
    —and congratulations.
CARETAKER: Thank you, comrade. [*Exit the CARETAKER,
    with her blunderbuss. The FOURTH OFFICIAL surveys the
    stage—the fallen monument, the crow on the table—then
    walks over to Karl Marx, looks him up and down, knowingly,
    and, with a smile, also exits, back into the Stalin statue.
    SEMYONOV looks gingerly about him, unfreezes, with a
    whistle of relief, and jumps off the plinth.*]
SEMYONOV: [*Coming forward to the audience*] What could I
    do? I ask you: what could I do? What would you have done?
    Kept quiet? Saved your skin? Lived to fight another day? Me
    too. Only just though.... [*Removing his wig, beard and sign.*]
    Poor Shukhov! Got the martyr quality, that guy. Who am I
    to stop him? He's a hero—believes in the constitution, Soviet
    legality. Well, let him find out about Soviet legality! OK, I
    could've warned him. Would he have listened? So what's the
    damage? He gets the chop: I get the story. 'Semyonov's Un-
    official History of the Russian Revolution: Chapter 703—The
    Martyrdom of Ivan Shukhov'! Fantastic! And complete with
    exhibits—crow, helmet, monument.... The monument! Jesus,
    they forgot the monument! [*He picks up the crow and*

helmet, then rushes to lift away the remains of the statue.]
Blast! S'nailed to the plinth! Don't trust anyone, these bureaucrats.... [*Throws the sack over his shoulder.*] Not to worry,
you'll hear from me in the end: I'm playing the long game,
see. [*He lifts the trapdoor and starts to climb down.*] Right
now, I've got to clear myself—testify against the hero.... [*As
he disappears.*] What's one more stone in a hailstorm? [*Tragic
music. Lights fade, picking out the deflated monument. Cut
music.*]

ACT THREE

SCENE ONE

*Music: the 'Promenade' from Mussorgsky's 'Pictures at an Exhibition'.
Up-stage, a bench and table; stage right, two tiny classroom chairs,
next to each other, with NATASHA and MOTHER SHUKHOV
sitting, waiting; a uniformed GUARD, smoking, beside them,
complete with rifle. On-screen, the Soviet flag and the legend:
THE PEOPLE VERSUS IVAN SHUKHOV. As the lights come
up, the GUARD—elderly, friendly—shuffles to his feet, puffing
at his cigarette.*

NATASHA: How much longer?

GUARD: [*Puffing*] Long as it takes.

NATASHA: We've been coming here for days.

GUARD: I've been coming here for years.

NATASHA: [*After a pause*] It's not right.

GUARD: Why belly-ache? You'll only get soap up your arse.

MOTHER SHUKHOV: [*To NATASHA*] Vanya's in enough trouble
as it is.

GUARD: [*Looking off-stage*] Aye, an' 'ere it comes.... Red 'ot,
this one, look you—bloody crimson. [*The GUARD smartens
himself up: he docks his cigarette, pops it into his rifle barrel.
Enter, the PROSECUTOR—small, icy, on his dignity, wearing
glasses, which he polishes repeatedly, and carrying a mass of
files.*]

PROSECUTOR: [*To the WOMEN*] Morning. [*To the GUARD*]
Morning. [*The GUARD snaps to attention and salutes.*]

GUARD: Court sergeant Protopopov—sir!

NATASHA: [*Jumping up and shouting*] It's not right! [*With his
saluting arm, the GUARD pushes her back down—then
resumes the salute.*]

PROSECUTOR: [*Stopping, taken aback*] I beg your pardon.

NATASHA: [*Jumping up again*] It's not right— [*As before, the
GUARD pushes her down.*]

GUARD: Sit down.

NATASHA: [*Held*] Keeping us waiting like this.

MOTHER SHUKHOV: Forgive her, Comrade Prosecutor—she's
upset.

PROSECUTOR: Naturally. [*He looks closely at NATASHA. The
GUARD releases his hold. NATASHA jumps up again.*]

NATASHA: [*Brave, frightened*] Dumb today, dead tomorrow!
   [*The GUARD looks helpless. The PROSECUTOR spins round.*]
MOTHER SHUKHOV: [*Pulling NATASHA back to her chair.*]
   Natalya!
PROSECUTOR: [*Coldly polite*] May I remind you that you are
   merely guests of this court?
MOTHER SHUKHOV: Surely, comrade, we are witnesses.
PROSECUTOR: The court has no need of witnesses.
NATASHA: [*Sarcastically*] A trial—without witnesses?
PROSECUTOR: This is not a trial: it is a hearing.
NATASHA: In secret? In the back of beyond? Who's going to
   hear?
PROSECUTOR: Precisely—it was felt a quiet proceeding would be
   best.
NATASHA: Who for?
PROSECUTOR: Your husband—his reputation.
NATASHA: My husband wanted an open trial. He's not afraid.
   Where's his lawyer?
PROSECUTOR: I am his lawyer.
NATASHA: [*Startled*] You're the prosecutor!
PROSECUTOR: Quite.
MOTHER SHUKHOV: [*With grave deference*] Can my son's def-
   ender also be his accuser?
PROSECUTOR: [*Smoothly*] Of course. It is the mark of a first-
   class mind.... Besides, your son is pleading guilty.
NATASHA: Never!
PROSECUTOR: I assure you—
NATASHA: Bastard!
GUARD: Wha-a-t? [*The GUARD grabs NATASHA and half lifts
   her from her chair.*]
NATASHA: [*Struggling defiantly*] That's why you've had him
   locked away for weeks on end, is it, starving him, beating him
   —to make him confess? [*The GUARD is trying to stifle NAT-
   ASHA's shouts.*]
MOTHER SHUKHOV: Natasha!
PROSECUTOR: It's all right, sergeant. [*The GUARD, looking
   perplexed, lets NATASHA fall back on to the chair.*] The
   prisoner Shukhov has confessed nothing: I have pleaded
   guilty on his behalf.
NATASHA: Why—if he hasn't confessed?
PROSECUTOR: The plea is guilty but insane. [*It takes a moment
   to register.*]
NATASHA: Insane? Where is he? Let me see him.
PROSECUTOR: Certainly. [*Calling off.*] Bring forward the prison-
   er. [*Enter, a white-uniformed NURSE. She pushes a wheelchair, strapped into which is IVAN, blanket over his legs,*]

straitjacket on, head swathed in bandages: his eyes are open but unseeing. The NURSE supports him at the back of the neck: MOTHER SHUKHOV screams silently.]

PROSECUTOR: Do not distress yourself, Comrade Shukhova. Your son has been ill. Surgery was required to relieve pressure on the brain. I am advised there is every hope of recovery. [*Meanwhile, NATASHA rises and approaches IVAN. From IVAN, no recognition.*]

NATASHA: Vanya? It's me—Natasha. It's all right, love, I'm here. What have they done to you? Vanya! [*She kisses him, gently, on the cheek. There is no response. Frightened, she steps back. Suddenly—cruelly—the NURSE lets IVAN's head drop to his chest, where it hangs, motionless.*] No! [*She backs away.*] No—o—o! [*MOTHER SHUKHOV takes her back to her chair and cradles her there—gazing fixedly at IVAN. The NURSE looks expressionlessly back.*]

PROSECUTOR: [*Clearing his throat*] Shall we proceed? [*No reply. Moving to the table, he begins throwing files upon it.*] The People versus Zhukov...The People versus Vukhov... Milyukov...Astarukhov...Shukhov. The People versus Shukhov ...Shukhov, Andrei Andreich...Basil Feodorovich...Fedya Lesnevich...Ivan Denisovich. [*Holding the last file, he turns, dramatically, to announce, in ringing tones.*] The People versus Ivan Denisovich Shukhov! [*Plop! Birdlime falls from above on to the PROSECUTOR's papers. With a frown up to the rafters, he looks at the GUARD—who suddenly leaps into action.*]

GUARD: [*Yelling*] The People versus Ivan D. Shukhov! [*The NURSE pulls IVAN's head upright. Enter, three JUDGES —all of middle age—a bewhiskered teacher, a cherubic farmer and a severe-looking woman. They sit at the bench.*]

FIRST JUDGE: No need to shout, Protopopov—we heard the first time. [*Fastidiously, the PROSECUTOR flicks the birdlime from his files with a handkerchief.*]

PROSECUTOR: [*Coldly*] This court is a disgrace. First, your sergeant smokes on duty. Second, the judiciary is unpunctual. Third, there appear to be birds nesting in the belfry.

FIRST JUDGE: A thousand pardons, Comrade Prosecutor—I'll have them removed at once.

PROSECUTOR: Later, later. Would you mind opening the proceedings?

FIRST JUDGE: Certainly. Number One Court, Melnitskoy District Kirov Province, is now in session. [*The FIRST JUDGE bangs his gavel on the table. The GUARD, jerking to attention, accidentally fires his rifle. The three JUDGES dive for cover under the table; MOTHER SHUKHOV pulls NATASHA closer; the NURSE and IVAN register nothing at all. The PROSECUTOR glares at the GUARD. From above, falls a large, dead crow. The lady JUDGE screams. The GUARD rushes over and picks up the crow.*]

GUARD: Got 'im! Mucky little 'orror! Besmirching the law!

FIRST JUDGE: Well done, sergeant.

GUARD: Thank you, your worship. [*The GUARD, plunging the bird inside his jacket, heads proudly back to his place.*]

PROSECUTOR: Sergeant—your cigarette....

GUARD: [*Stopped in his tracks*] Sir? [*The PROSECUTOR picks up the GUARD's cigarette butt and holds it out to him.*] Yes, sir- -much obliged, sir. [*The GUARD resumes position, looks from the fag-end to the gun, but shoves the butt behind his ear.*]

PROSECUTOR: May we begin?

FIRST JUDGE: By all means.

PROSECUTOR: [*Nervous but reasonable, even concerned*] Honoured Judges, the manifold errors of the former athlete, Shukhov, culminate in a major breach of Section Thirteen of the Security Act, 1929, to whit a letter, found on his person and intended for communication to foreign powers, containing the gravest treasons and calumnies against the State. Comrades, the spirit of patriotism cries out for exemplary punishment. But may I remind you: only a year ago the prisoner Shukhov was a hero, the very symbol of Russian manhood, courage and revolutionary purpose. The prosecution seeks no vengeance here. The State is prepared to accept, in mitigation of his crimes, that Shukhov became the dupe of conspiracy against the revolution, while the balance of his mind was disturbed. He pleads guilty but insane. And the prosecution accepts that plea. In fact, I am instructed in all humanity to substantiate it- -the prisoner himself being incapable, after surgery, of addressing the court.... [*The PROSECUTOR turns to NATASHA and MOTHER SHUKHOV.*] Hence this quiet hearing, outside the capital—to avoid upsetting him. [*Again no response.*] Comrades, I shall call no witnesses for the defence. Instead, I shall, with your permission, enter tape-recorded affidavits, establishing beyond doubt that the former hero, Shukhov, is suffering—and I quote—from 'paranoid schizophrenia—'

NATASHA: [*Quietly*] Liar.

PROSECUTOR: [*Without faltering*] '—with associated persecution fantasies and delusions of guilt, aggravated by an acute castration complex—'

NATASHA: [*Louder*] Liar.

PROSECUTOR: [*Pauses, eyebrows raised, then continues.*] '—a condition of both subjective and objective violence, manifesting itself in an urge to self-destruction, which can be relieved only by a prolonged period of rest and treatment at a State sanitorium for the mentally unwell.'

NATASHA: [*Finally yelling*] Liar! Liar! Liar!

PROSECUTOR: I beg your pardon. [*The GUARD puts a restraining hand on NATASHA's shoulder. She shrugs him off.*]

NATASHA: What about the drugs, then?

PROSECUTOR: [*Off-hand*] Drugs?

NATASHA: [*Rushing to the bench*] Ask him, Your Honour. It's all because of the drugs.

PROSECUTOR: [*Dismissive*] You're as mad as he is.

NATASHA: He's not mad! [*To the bench again.*] Look how they've beaten him! Look what they've done to him!

PROSECUTOR: Very well—he's not mad: he's a traitor. Choose! Would you like him shot?

NATASHA: [*To judges*] I want him freed.

PROSECUTOR: Out of the question.

NATASHA: I want him free!

FIRST JUDGE: [*Banging his gavel*] Silence!

IVAN: [*Chillingly*] Brodsky!

[*Blackout. Cut screen-picture. Immediately, the stage is full of the sound of the mine-collapse from Act One—rising to a crescendo. In the darkness, through the noise, IVAN cries again.*] Brodsky!

SCENE TWO

Spotlight on IVAN, still in the wheelchair. The NURSE, unable to calm him, shouts into her pocket-communicator.

NURSE: Emergency! Emergency!

[*Lights full up. On-screen, the barbed wire fence and watchtowers of a prison-camp hospital. Enter the asylum deputy, VANITSIN, also three white-coated ATTENDANTS, pushing a bed and carrying a vast battery, with cranking handle and attached headset, for electrotherapy. The ATTENDANTS fall upon IVAN, stifle him, gag him, whip off his bandages and fix the electrodes on his cropped head. VANITSIN gives the handle a whir. IVAN stiffens, then relaxes, smiling through the gag.*]

VANITSIN: Leonid—post-operative condition. [*The FIRST ATTENDANT checks IVAN's pulse, peers into his eyes.*]

FIRST ATTENDANT: No convulsion. Pulse normal. Eyes twinkling.

VANITSIN: Strange. I checked the battery myself. Take out the gag. [*The FIRST ATTENDANT obliges. IVAN grins merrily.*] All right, Shukhov--what's so funny?

IVAN: I keep hearing voices.

VANITSIN: [*Furious*] We'll soon put a stop to that! [*VANITSIN whirs the crank handle violently: the machine bangs. VANITSIN and his ATTENDANTS drop. IVAN roars with laughter. Enter, hurrying, DOCTOR VERA LYUBOVNA, a ripely attractive woman of about thirty.*]

VERA: How dare you?
[*IVAN stops laughing. VANITSIN and the ATTENDANTS get sheepishly to their feet.*]

VANITSIN: Director's orders. [*VERA pulls off the electrodes, feels IVAN's forehead, then turns on VANITSIN.*]

VERA: Shukhov is my patient. Kindly put him back to bed. [*The ATTENDANTS await instructions.*]

VANITSIN: You heard the doctor. [*He hands VERA the clipboard and marches out.*] I shall file a complaint. [*The NURSE and ATTENDANTS unstrap IVAN from the chair, cart him bodily across to the bed and hurl him on to it.*]

NURSE: One, two, three—heave!
[*The bed jack-knifes, with a crash, leaving IVAN in the ruins. Totally unconcerned, the NURSE and ATTENDANTS exit, taking the wheelchair, battery, etc.*]

VERA: [*Writing*] Pity about that.

IVAN: [*Ruefully*] There's a bottleneck in beds.

VERA: You should have been asleep. Bad dreams?

IVAN: Where am I?

VERA: Another hospital. You've been very ill.

IVAN: Where's Natasha? [*Pause*] My wife, Natasha—where is she? [*IVAN tries to raise himself on the bed ruins.*] Can't bloody move!

VERA: [*Casually*] You *were* rather violent.

IVAN: [*Quietly*] Bitch! [*Shouting*] Lousy, stinking bitch! [*He rolls off the broken bed, gets up on to his knees, arms pinioned, and scrabbles towards VERA, toppling over at her feet.*]

VERA: [*Taunting*] Come and get me, then. Come on, Shukhov, get the bitch! Let's have it—all that pain, all that hate--give it me, Shukhov, give it me, give it me! [*IVAN roars with frustration: VERA shouts over him.*] Or you'll be bound like this for ever! [*IVAN spits at her. VERA slaps his face. IVAN bellows with laughter. VERA turns aside, throws the clipboard on to the bed, and faces him again.*] All right, here's the truth. [*She speaks slowly, deliberately*] It's an asylum. Your mother is confined to her village. Your wife— [*She hesitates.*] your wife is in a work camp—in Siberia—for abusing the court at

71

your trial. [*IVAN holds VERA's look, then howls with pain.*]

IVAN: Bastards! [*Baying now.*] Let me out! Let me out!

VERA: What's wrong, Mr Universe? Jacket too tight? Shall I slacken it for you? [*Disdainfully, VERA unfastens the top laces of the straitjacket. IVAN twists, struggles to loosen the rest and cannot.*] How weak you are! The immortal Shukhov —caught, like a butterfly in a net. [*Unfastening the other laces.*] And only I can set him free again--for his one frail season in the world....

IVAN: [*Fiercely*] In a nuthouse! [*He rips off the straitjacket and hurls it aside.*]

VERA: [*Laughing*] Where you belong.

IVAN: Ballocks!

VERA: People in their right minds do not oppose the State.

IVAN: Bullshit!

VERA: It's a small price to pay.

IVAN: What for?

VERA: The time being...

IVAN: Oh sure, till tomorrow. Tomorrow we're dead.

VERA: Don't you believe in tomorrow?

IVAN: I did—once. [*He limps across to the bed and sits in the ruins.*]

VERA: But not any more.

IVAN: How can I? When I wake up, it's always today. Then I get to wonderin' what happened yesterday.

VERA: [*With calm certainty*] Yesterday, we made the revolution, comrade: we seized the land and fought to keep it: we raised our people from their knees—we gave them back their hope. [*IVAN rolls over.*]

IVAN: Glory hallelujah!

VERA: [*Approaching him*] Today, Shukhov: no one starves--not in Russia. Every man has work and a roof to his head. No one is exploited: our women are free: our children are safe. Moscow will never burn again! Tomorrow, the people will choose their future! Tomorrow, the revolution will be theirs!

IVAN: Suppose tomorrow never comes.

VERA: Tomorrow is inevitable.

IVAN: Says who?

VERA: The Party.

IVAN: [*Bitter*] I'm not a member of the Party.

VERA: Who's fault is that?

IVAN: It's never anybody's fault! [*Jumping off the bed, he grabs VERA and pulls her head back by the hair.*] Here, now, if I hurt you—who's to blame? Who's to blame? [*IVAN throws her down beside the bed.*] Me! I'm to blame. Aren't I? [*Ashamed, he comes to her, touches her head.*] Sorry.

[*VERA looks at him—then gets up, straightens her coat, retrieves the clipboard.*]

VERA: Forget it.

IVAN: I said I was sorry.

VERA: [*Making notes*] Sorry's not enough, Mr Universe. You can't just be 'sorry' about a revolution.

IVAN: It's not the revolution that's hurting us! Not any more....
[*VERA sighs, puts away her pen, seems about to leave. IVAN picks up the straitjacket, challenges her with it. Fiercely...*]
Is this the revolution?

VERA: If necessary.
[*Pause.*]

IVAN: You mean it, don't you?

VERA: Why not?

IVAN: Because it's a lie!

VERA: Shukhov, you're a child. Where've you been all your life!

IVAN: The Garden of fuckin' Eden! [*He sits down again, on the broken bed.*]

VERA: Eat your apple, then, like a good boy. Go on. Just one more bite.... Save yourself.

IVAN: [*Derisive*] How?

VERA: Admit you were wrong.

IVAN: I wasn't wrong.

VERA: [*Gently*] Does it really matter? I'm trying to help you. It'll be all right—in the end. Believe me!

IVAN: I don't even bloody understand you.

VERA: [*Mocking*] Because I'm a woman?

IVAN: What's that got to do with it?

VERA: Because I've got long hair and soft breasts?

IVAN: No.

VERA: [*Confronting him, unbuttoning her coat*] Like to kiss my breasts, would you?

IVAN: No.

VERA: Like to lay your head there and have a good cry?

IVAN: Get stuffed!

VERA: I do.

IVAN: I'm glad! I'm bloody glad!
[*Pause*]

VERA: [*Shrugging*] Fine—stick around...and suffer.

IVAN: [*Quietly, puzzled*] It moved.

VERA: What?

IVAN: [*Elated*] It moved! [*IVAN is gazing raptly at his groin, penis clutched in both hands.*]

VERA: [*More notes*] High noon! Patient re-erected.

IVAN: Just a tremble.

VERA: What did a prick ever prove?

73

IVAN: While there's life, there's hope.

[*Enter at a rush, the ASYLUM DIRECTOR, with his deputy, VANITSIN, flanked by NURSE and ATTENDANTS. The DIRECTOR—cynical, courteous—takes in the scene at a glance.*]

DIRECTOR: What exactly is going on here?

IVAN: [*Blithely*] Bugger all!

DIRECTOR: Doctor Lyubovna, I asked a question.

VERA: [*Braving it out*] Change of treatment, comrade Director.

DIRECTOR: Fascinating! And the nature of this psychiatric revisionism?

VERA: [*Laughing, ironic*] Love! [*Sniggers*]

DIRECTOR: Love? Doctor, I have studied the entire canon of Soviet psychoanalysis—to say nothing of the complete works of Marx and Engels—without once coming across the word. Comrade Lenin may have mentioned it in a footnote: if so, it has escaped my attention. Comrade Stalin, you may recall, discouraged the very use of the term, as lacking objective reality. Your treatment, therefore, is at an end, doctor: kindly adjourn to my room. [*Glances among the ATTENDANTS and NURSES.*] And in future, please do not neglect the regulation under-garment. [*VERA exits. IVAN crawls off the bed wreckage.*]

IVAN: Nearly a nasty accident....

DIRECTOR: Yesterday, Shukhov, you may have been the strongest man in the world: today you are less than one millionth of one per cent of the Soviet nation. You are statistically insignificant—you are probably not entitled to a bed at all. Yet you have squashed three that we know of and sliced up a vintage four-poster, complete with curtains and commode. In future, you will sleep on the floor.

IVAN: Old Nikolai—he knew the score.

DIRECTOR: [*Checking number*] Patient 99291! While deploring Doctor Lyubovna's methods, I accept your readiness for the second stage of cure...work according to aptitude. You shall be a clerk, in our records section—one of our purpose-built labourers' huts. Do not try to escape: the security system is foolproof. In the event of your death, I am instructed your body will revert to the State, for medical research—as quid pro quo, no doubt, for the beds. Vanitsin, a uniform, if you please.

VANITSIN: We've run out...of uniforms.

DIRECTOR: Improvise, man!

VANITSIN: [*In a panic*] Yes, sir. Right away, sir. [*He begins running on the spot.*] Ready everyone? [*The NURSE and ATTENDANTS join in.*] Follow me! [*He leads them off-*

stage. *IVAN makes to go with them, but the DIRECTOR drags him back.*]

DIRECTOR: Not you, Shukhov.

[*Immediately, VANITSIN, NURSE and ATTENDANTS re-appear, each carrying a large pot of paint and a brush.*]

VANITSIN: Patient 99291—attention! Arms stretch! Legs apart!

[*IVAN obeys. Loud, heroic music. VANITSIN, NURSE and ATTENDANTS proceed to paint black prisoner's stripes on to IVAN's pyjamas. Cut music. Job done, NURSE and ATTENDANTS exit, at the double. Lights cut to spot around IVAN. The DIRECTOR, taking VANITSIN's brush, adds the finishing touches—then steps back to admire his handiwork.*]

DIRECTOR: Brilliant! [*IVAN relaxes.*] Stand still, man—you're not dry! [*Exit the DIRECTOR and VANITSIN. Another burst of music. IVAN is seen, stretched, frozen, striped—as the last image before blackout.*]

SCENE THREE

Towards rear-stage, centre, three double bunks, covered in graffiti, arranged as three sides of a square, open to the audience. Candles at the bunk-ends. Low light, down-stage, reveals IVAN, in prison uniform, crouching, holding a catapult. All at once he takes aim and fires—into the flies.

IVAN: Got 'im! [*A big, black crow falls plumb at the feet of PETROV, entering, in barber's gear.*]

PETROV: Cor, stone the crows! [*PETROV's face is horribly dis-figured by skin grafts, which have twisted his mouth, distort-ing his voice. Looking from crow to IVAN and back again, he finally picks the bird up.*] D'you do that?

IVAN: Yeah.

PETROV: What with?

IVAN: [*Showing the weapon*] Catapult.

PETROV: Catapult?

IVAN: Sure. Learnt to pot crows when I wer' a kid.

PETROV: Where d'yer find a catapult in a loony bin?

IVAN: Made it. Look. Knife an' fork from chow; boot tongue; piece of elastic an' one pebble—clean through't breast.

PETROV: [*Throwing the bird across to IVAN*] Are you Shukhov?

IVAN: Yes. [*He pockets the catapult and the crow. Stiffly, PETROV moves towards him, smiling.*]

PETROV: Petrov—camp barber. [*Handshake.*]

IVAN: This hut ten? They said report to hut ten.

PETROV: Did they now? You're a bit big fer 'ut ten. Come on,
I'll show you round. [*Lights full up, revealing the bunks. On-
screen: barbed-wire stockades, observation towers. The two
men enter the hut. PETROV takes a shaving bag from under
his pillow, hangs a mirror from the bunk-end, takes off his
apron, then, gingerly, his shirt. Large parts of his torso and
arms are covered in the same terrible scars. Flaunting...*]
Pretty, aren't I?

IVAN: [*Horrified*] Strewth!

PETROV: Tattoos, see. Tattoos not allowed!

IVAN: I've got tattoos.

PETROV: Where? [*IVAN shows his arms: PETROV snorts.*] Kid's
stuff!

IVAN: They altered 'em. [*PETROV examines IVAN's arm closely,
then lets it fall.*]

PETROV: You wer' lucky, mate. They chopped mine out. Thirty-
seven tattoos- -bloody 'orse butchers! They've 'ad enough
skin off me to start a lampshade fac'try. Five 'undred
stitches! Tell you, there's a tart down't laundry, likes lickin'
scars, no kid—just beggin' fer it, she is, arse like an apple: but
they've got me stitched that tight, if I screwed 'er, I'd split...
mucky all 'er sheets. [*PETROV has turned away again and is
stropping an open razor, on a leather. IVAN, squatting on his
haunches, watches him.*] Want yer eyes peeled?

IVAN: [*Taken aback*] No.

PETROV: Quit starin', then.

IVAN: [*Grinning*] Stroppy sod, aren't you?

PETROV: 'Nother thing: don't mek jokes.

IVAN: Why?

PETROV: It 'urts when I laugh.

IVAN: [*Warming to him*] What 'appens when you cry?

PETROV: Can't.

IVAN: What?

PETROV: Cry. 'Aven't cried fer years—sin' they sawed off mi
eyelids. Can't even blink. Sleep wi' mi eyes open. [*PETROV
has started shaving—with the bare razor—no soap—all very
painstaking.*]

IVAN: Why don't you use soap?

PETROV: So's I can see where I'm goin'.

IVAN: [*Pacing*] I've got to get out of here! We've all got to get
out of here!

PETROV: [*Still shaving*] Do us a favour, eh? 'Eroes don't get out:
they get their 'uts a bad name.

IVAN: What do we do, then? Curl up an' die?

PETROV: Fight the buggers! Dun't matter 'ow—just keep fightin'.
Taraschenko—all 'ee wants is to go home. He's a Tartar, my

76

bunker, from't Crimea: 'is folk wer' transported—dumped in't snow-country- thousands of 'em. Least pip squeak nah an' they're arrested. S'how Taraschenko got nicked. An' he's never said another word since. Not a dickey bird. Sod 'em, he's thinkin': whatever they do, in 'ere [*Patting his chest.*] I defy the bastards!

IVAN: And you? [*PETROV wipes his face, stows his tackle, gestures to IVAN for help with his shirt.*]

PETROV: Me? Soft as a spinster's tit. Never 'armed no one: never cheated, never stole, never rich, never went to church, drank a bit, mebbe, wenched some—who 'asn't? But I'm just a ghost in't bloody machine! 'Prisoner 63529 double one stroke B beggin' permission to spew, sir!' If ther's nowt in it fer me, fuck it! I'm only human. [*From off-stage, the sound of an iron bar being struck repeatedly with a hammer.*] Oi, oi, clockin' off. Lads'll be back soon. [*He arranges blankets on the bunks. IVAN sits on the edge of PETROV's bed, pulling out the crow's feathers.*]

IVAN: [*Quietly*] Petrov—how did it happen?

PETROV: Builder, aren't I? One day, trouble on't site: bloke gets knifed: police rope everybody in. Bang—Petrov's got a record. Next job—railways. Some burk's floggin' picks 'n shovels to a road gang. Oi, that Petrov, 'ee's got form. Bang—work camp, two years 'ard. Who, me? What for? Bang--solit'ry: Czar's old clink in Moscow—ounce o' meat, four ounce o' bread an' a cup o' water a day. So what do I do? Bloody fight 'em. Wi' tattoos. Picked up tattooin' in't Navy. 'Fuck Marxist-Leninism'! On mi for'ead, chest, arms, anywhere. Bang—tattoos forbidden! State Insult! Anti-Soviet propaganda! Cut 'em out! 'Cept every time they cut one out, I do another—on mi feet, be'ind mi knees. An' they allers find 'em: keep cuttin' 'em out an' stretchin't skin to cover t'oles, till I can 'ardly walk or talk or piss or 'owt. So I conned 'em proper. Laid off a shade, till they thought I'd given up an' shoved me in 'ere. Then I did one they cun't find. [*Suddenly, he drops his pants and bends, as best he can, showing his bare arse to IVAN.*] Every time I'm sittin' there, I'm thinking: 'I'm not dun yet, yer scum, I'm not dun yet!' [*Enter, laughing raucously, DIMSHITS, the hut orderly. Behind him, the hut occupants straggle in from work. On-screen: close-up picture of thick strands of barbed wire.*]

DIMSHITS: Always took you for a bum-boy, Petrov! [*PETROV pulls up his pants, cursing under his breath, and retreats to his bunk. IVAN shoves the crow back into his jacket. To the other inmates...*] Come on Genghis Khan, look lively--you, too, Tolstoi. 'Ey, Jesus, it's the third day—no 'angin' about.

[*The inmates do not react to IVAN.*] Right, you lot, stand
by your beds. That's more like it. Nah, got a surprise for you.
From here on, you'll be *seven* dwarfs! [*Sudden silence.
Finally, the hut-leader, KOTELIANSKY, a dignified, bearded,
Jewish scientist, replies.*]

KOTELIANSKY: You can't.

DIMSHITS: Why not?

KOTELIANSKY: Regulations.

DIMSHITS: [*Slyly*] What regulations?

KOTELIANSKY: Six beds to a hut. We're full up.

DIMSHITS: Course you are, clever cunt! This nut's special: he
kips on the floor.

KOTELIANSKY: [*On his mettle*] Out of the question.

DIMSHITS: Why?

GAVRILOV: Rats 'll get him.

DIMSHITS: [*Swinging round*] You're the only rat round 'ere,
Tolstoi. My huts 're clean.

KOVALCHUK: We having a Red Cross inspection?

DIMSHITS: [*Grabbing KOVALCHUK by the throat.*] Cheeky
little swine!

IVAN: [*Quietly*] Leave him alone. [*DIMSHITS stops dead.
Silence.*]

DIMSHITS: Blimey, it talks.

IVAN: [*Firmer*] I said leave him alone.

DIMSHITS: I heard you, Shukhov. Keep your knickers on.
[*DIMSHITS lets go of KOVALCHUK. Immediately, PET-
LIURA—a fiery Ukrainian with cropped hair and a patch on
one eye—runs to IVAN.*]

PETLIURA: Ivan Shukhov? Man, you can have my bed.

DIMSHITS: No chance: he might squash your bugs. 'Sides, it's
Director's orders.

KOTELIANSKY: Is that so?

IVAN: [*Awkward*] Yes. [*KOTELIANSKY approaches IVAN.*]

KOTELIANSKY: [*Sympathetically*] We gathered they'd brought
you here. I am Abram Koteliansky. [*Peering around, over his
glasses.*] They call me Einstein... [*Wryly*] I had hoped to
take my family to Israel. Welcome to hut ten.

DIMSHITS: [*Interrupting*] Politicals for the re'abilitation of!
[*KOTELIANSKY ignores him. He and IVAN shake hands.*]

IVAN: Thank you.

KOTELIANSKY: [*Making the introductions*] This is Nikki Petliu
Petliura, our Ukrainian nationalist. [*IVAN grins: they
embrace.*] The writer, Gavrilov—perhaps you've heard of him?
His documents on the terror, his *Book of the Dead*....

GAVRILOV: [*Drily*] They're out of print.

KOTELIANSKY: Pavel Kovalchuk.... Pavel is a Baptist. I assume

78

you know the State's way with Baptists.

KOVALCHUK: God go with you.

KOTELIANSKY: Anton Taraschenko....

IVAN: [*Smiling*] Hello.

KOTELIANSKY: Petrov you've already met.

DIMSHITS: OK, cut the crap!

KOTELIANSKY: [*Blithely*] Piotr Dimshits, nurse in charge, huts ten to fifteen, black marketeer extraordinary.

IVAN: D'you ever work in Moscow?

DIMSHITS: [*Sly*] That's my brother.... Right, lads, shop's open! [*DIMSHITS throws wide his greatcoat: its many inside pockets are bulging with goods. Immediate activity. KOVALCHUK climbs on to a top bunk and begins reading his Bible.*]

KOTELIANSKY: Gold ring.

DIMSHITS: Trust a Jew.

KOTELIANSKY: [*Softly*] Take it or leave it.

DIMSHITS: [*Delving into his coat*] Tobacco—four tins.

KOTELIANSKY: Done. [*They exchange. KOTELIANSKY retreats to his bunk and lights up a pipe.*]

PETROV: [*From his bed*] One shoe.

DIMSHITS: What would I do with one shoe?

PETROV: No idea. What would you do with two balls? [*Laughter*]

DIMSHITS: You're barred! [*PETROV grins, gives him a 'V' sign and sinks back on his bunk.*]

PETLIURA: Pin up.

DIMSHITS: Let's see. [*Appraising the picture, he makes his offer.*] Jar of vaseline.

PETLIURA: [*Putting the picture away*] Filthy sod!

GAVRILOV: [*Coming forward*] Monkey wrench.

DIMSHITS: Not another monkey wrench. 'Ere, where you gettin' 'em from?

GAVRILOV: Depends where you're selling them. [*More laughter.*]

DIMSHITS: [*Mock outrage*] Tolstoi, you're bent! Swallow a nail, you'd shit a corkscrew.

GAVRILOV: I'd prefer a pound of tea.

DIMSHITS: Indian?

GAVRILOV: China.

DIMSHITS: Half a pound. [*Grudgingly*] An' a cup o' sugar.

GAVRILOV: Done. [*They exchange.*]

DIMSHITS: Any more for any more? [*Pause. He starts to fasten his coat.*]

IVAN: Crow. [*All eyes on IVAN.*]

DIMSHITS: Come again. [*IVAN pulls out the crow and pushes it in DIMSHITS' face.*]

IVAN: Crow!

DIMSHITS: Dildo! [*Reaches into his coat. IVAN throws the crow at DIMSHITS' feet.*]

IVAN: Eat it! [*DIMSHITS pockets both crow and dildo.*]

DIMSHITS: You'll be eatin' crow before we've finished, Shukhov.

IVAN: You'll never be finished with me!

DIMSHITS: Jesus, lend him your mattress till tomorrow. Be good, now: don't do anything I wouldn't do. [*Silence. KOVAL-CHUK intent on his Bible. PETROV capers into the middle of the hut, holding the plucked crow-feathers at the back of his head, like a Red Indian.*]

PETROV: [*Whooping*] Geronimo! [*Laughter. But not from IVAN. He moves to PETROV, takes the feathers, examines them.*]

IVAN: What did you say?

PETROV: [*Puzzled*] Geronimo....

IVAN: [*A revelation*] Yes—yes! Geronimo! Listen, do you want to help me?

PETROV: I can't help misself. 'Ow can I 'elp you?

IVAN: With these feathers, whittled down to fine points. With inks from the print shop. With tattoos, Petrov—tattoos!

PETROV: [*Appalled*] Are yer blind? Din't yer see? [*Tears open his shirt.*] This is what they do wi' tattoos.

IVAN: [*Triumphantly*] Not if you cover your whole body—all at once. They'd have to flay me alive!

PETROV: God almighty!

[*Pause*]

KOTELIANSKY: You're not serious?

IVAN: Try me.

KOTELIANSKY: Why, Shukhov—why do you want to disfigure yourself?

IVAN: [*With a cry*] I'm crippled! What good's my body any more —'cept to fight with? I want a body that fits my life—like before, when I was free. Free! The State's put a ticket on me: the day I die, they're gonna saw me up an' stick me in bottles. Well, I want to laugh in their bloody faces! Long as I'm alive, I want my body to say: this is Ivan Shukhov—free, in a mad-house. I've got it all worked out. I want to be a picture o' the revolution!

[*Pause*]

KOTELIANSKY: [*Slowly*] You know you'd be punished?

IVAN: Yes.

KOTELIANSKY: And Petrov, too—he'd be punished.

PETROV: Bugger that!

KOTELIANSKY: [*Still weighing it all up*] Another thing: the operation would take time—we'd need a look-out system: other hut-members would be involved—and subject to reprisals. I cannot allow any plan without their approval. [*Solemnly*] Nikki?

PETLIURA: [*Unhesitating*] If that's what he wants. We're in it together.

KOTELIANSKY: Jesus?

KOVALCHUK: [*Reading*] Mmm?

KOTELIANSKY: Kovalchuk, please put down your book.

KOVALCHUK: It's not a book: it's the Bible.

KOTELIANSKY: Do you agree to Shukhov's plan?

KOVALCHUK: Of course. I shall pray for him.

KOTELIANSKY: Tolstoi?

GAVRILOV: On one condition. Any words and I help choose them.

IVAN: Done!

KOTELIANSKY: Taraschenko?

TARASCHENKO: [*Long pause.*] It is Comrade Shukhov's affair. [*He smiles: there is a roar of laughter.*]

KOTELIANSKY: The oracle hath spoken! We are agreed. Let Shukhov be anointed! [*They crowd round IVAN, eagerly. PETLIURA exits. Lights slowly down. Cut screen picture. KOVALCHUK lights candles. IVAN sits on the floor, his back to the audience; KOTELIANSKY and TARASCHENKO hold his arms out; PETROV works on IVAN's shoulders. The candles keep them in silhouette. KOVALCHUK is reading his Bible; GAVRILOV is on guard at the door. Silence.*]

IVAN: [*Yelling out.*] Aaagh!

PETROV: Quit wrigglin'.... [*PETROV works on. Again IVAN cries, this time his head thrown back in agony, as KOTEL-IANSKY and TARASCHENKO hold him.*]

IVAN: Aaagh!

GAVRILOV: Gag him, can't you?

KOTELIANSKY: [*Worried*] Leave the rest, Vanya.

IVAN: No!

KOTELIANSKY: [*Appealing*] Petrov!

PETROV: S'nearly done.

KOTELIANSKY: He's burning.... You'll kill him.

PETROV: [*Possessed*] Where's Nikki wi' that red? Must 'ave more red.

IVAN: [*Another howl*] Aaagh! [*He passes out. PETROV contin-ues. KOVALCHUK crosses himself, praying. TARASCHEN-KO wipes IVAN's face with a cloth.*]

GAVRILOV: Christ, he'll wake the whole camp!

KOTELIANSKY: Petrov, I order you to stop.

PETROV: [*Unheeding*] Where the hell is Petliura?

GAVRILOV: [*Shrilly*] Shh! [*Frozen silence.... At last*] S'all right. It's Nikki.

KOTELIANSKY: Thank the Lord. [*Enter, PETLIURA, running, bent double, with a phial of ink. PETROV lights another candle on the floor.*]

PETROV: Where've you bin?

PETLIURA: Couldn't crack the lock.

PETROV: Ne'er mind. 'Old 'im tight!

KOTELIANSKY: I forbid it.

PETROV: Month's work: one corner left—corner o' one wing. When he comes round, who's gonna tell 'im it's not done?

KOTELIANSKY: [*Thinking it over*] Two more minutes! [*PETROV opens the ink-phial, chooses a new quill.*]

PETROV: [*Angrily*] Wrong shade. Wrong bloody shade!

KOTELIANSKY: Who's going to notice?

PETROV: It'll be ruined!

PETLIURA: Signing it, are you? [*IVAN moans.*]

GAVRILOV: [*Suddenly*] Enemy—port beam!

KOTELIANSKY: Heading this way?

GAVRILOV: One of the doctors.

PETLIURA: [*Scornful*] After midnight?

GAVRILOV: [*Peering*] It's a woman! Sticking to the walls—out of the lights.

KOTELIANSKY: [*Desperate*] How much more?

PETROV: Touch o' blue.

PETLIURA: [*Rushing to the door*] Who is it?

GAVRILOV: Lyubnova.

PETLIURA: [*Confirming*] Coming here.

KOTELIANSKY: [*Looking round at everyone*] What for?

PETROV: [*Elated*] Let her come! Let 'em all come! [*Hectic activity. PETROV shakes IVAN, taking his head in his hands, babbling in his ears—as KOTELIANSKY and TARASCHENKO let go of his arms.*] Shukhov, wake up! D'you hear? It's finished!

GAVRILOV: [*From the door*] Fifteen seconds.

PETLIURA: Get him off the floor. [*IVAN is naked. KOTELIANSKY, TARASCHENKO and PETLIURA ease him upright. PETROV tears plasters from IVAN's forehead and face, making him start awake with pain.*]

GAVRILOV: Ten seconds!

KOTELIANSKY: [*Praying*] God of Abraham, God of Isaac....

IVAN: [*Swaying, as they hold him*] What's wrong?

PETLIURA: Lyubovna's here.

PETROV: Douse the candles! [*Stage momentarily in darkness, as the flames are snuffed.*]

GAVRILOV: Five, four, three, two, one, zero! [*KOVALCHUK closes his Bible. In the centre-stage group, PETROV, now an avenging master-of-ceremonies, manoeuvres IVAN into facing*

the door. The rest become a kind of welcoming committee.
On zero, VERA enters, spotlit: GAVRILOV comes forward
to bar her way.]

VERA: I'd like to see the patient, Shukhov—I've a message for him.

GAVRILOV: [Moving aside] Doctor Lyubovna, to see Comrade
Shukhov. [Suddenly lights full up. The screen is black. PET-
ROV releases IVAN. VERA sees before her the fevered,
apparently sightless, tottering figure. She stops dead. IVAN
is covered, almost from head to foot, in tattoos. His chest and
stomach are completely filled with lines of tiny, close writing;
his back is resplendent with a huge red admiral butterfly; on
his forehead, in large letters—'I am a free man'; his arms and
legs bear more of the tattoo text, his buttocks carry the hammer and sickle symbols. Achieved mainly, perhaps, by a decor-
ated body stocking.]

VERA: Oh no! For mercy's sake, no!

PETROV: Allow me to introduce the New Man: revolution incarnate—the future made flesh! [He turns IVAN round like some
dreadful fashion model.]

VERA: Leave him alone! Leave him alone, you monster! [She
rushes at PETROV pushing him aside. IVAN staggers again
—she has to stop him falling...she has to touch him.]

IVAN: I'm blind! [Appalled, VERA backs away from him. IVAN
sways towards her, cannot find her. Crying his name, she pulls
a blanket from one of the bunks, runs to him and wraps it
round him: he winces at the lightest touch.]

VERA: Shukhov! [Clutching the blanket, IVAN totters back to
face the audience. VERA turns on the other prisoners: coldly
now...] Who did this to him?

PETROV: Crows' quills an' printer's ink. Fancy 'im, do yer? Luvly
piece o' work! [VERA shouts into a pocket communicator.]

VERA: Guards! Hut ten! [Siren: a long loud blast. The INMATES
approach IVAN.]

KOTELIANSKY: [Shaking IVAN's hand] Goodbye, Shukhov.

IVAN: [Unable to see him] Goodbye?

GAVRILOV: Good luck.

PETLIURA: Stay free.

KOVALCHUK: God bless.

IVAN: God bless?

TARASCHENKO: The great Shukhov! [IVAN is turning, side to
side, trying to make sense of them all. Finally, PETROV embraces him.]

PETROV: Remember me.
    [From left and right, SOLDIERS enter, with guns: DIMSHITS
    scurries behind them.]

VERA: Arrest these men! [The SOLDIERS bundle the INMATES

83

against the bunks, searching them, rough-handling them. There is no resistance. In the mêlée, a SOLDIER grabs IVAN from behind, in a neck-hold: IVAN crumples in his grasp, crying out in pain.]

IVAN: Aaagh!

VERA: [*Quickly*] Not that one: leave him to me. [*Doubtfully, the SOLDIER releases his grip: IVAN slips to the floor: VERA kneels to him.*]

PETROV: [*Shouting*] Mind the bleedin' butterfly! [*Brutally, he is smashed down with a gun butt.*]

VERA: Take them away. [*The INMATES are led and pushed off-stage—PETROV, unconscious, dragged by the armpits. DIM-SHITS follows, re-pocketing his goods. Silence. VERA and IVAN are alone.*] Why, Shukhov? Why did you do it?

IVAN: [*Stirring*] Natasha? Is that you? Have they let you go?

VERA: Shukhov—it's Vera Lyubovna.

IVAN: I—I can't see.... Natasha—where are you?

VERA: [*Holding him*] Here. I'm here.

IVAN: Don't leave me.

VERA: [*Steeling herself*] Shukhov, your wife is in prison now: your mother's been arrested: something's happened. [*Looking around.*] I came to tell you. [*Pause*]

IVAN: I'm free now, Natasha. They'll never catch me again. I've made myself strong for you. Say you still love me.

VERA: I love you.

IVAN: We can go home now—to Sheremestvo.

VERA: Yes...to Sheremestvo.

IVAN: There's a house in the square....

VERA: Yes, Vanya.

IVAN: You're so beautiful.

VERA: Am I?

IVAN: [*Falling unconscious*] Oh yes—so beautiful....

VERA: And you...so beautiful. [*Still kneeling, VERA holds IVAN —waiting. Enter, the DIRECTOR, with two GUARDS. VERA does not even look up.*]

DIRECTOR: [*Icily*] Congratulations, doctor, on uncovering this vile affair. [*Silently, VERA is weeping. Blackout.*]

SCENE FOUR

During the blackout, repeated loud clanging noises, as of iron doors banging shut. Then on-screen, the butterfly tattooed on IVAN's back. Spotlight, stage right—upon IVAN, lying unconscious, the blanket thrown over him. He twitches painfully awake,

84

*stirs, feels the striped prison clothes beside him and dresses him-
self: he finds his catapult, which he begins to dismantle, kneeling,
singing, in an odd cracked voice.*

IVAN: [*Singing*]

> If you dance then you will need
> boots of shining leather,
> money in your pocket-book,
> in your cap a feather....

[*The song tails off. IVAN gazes out at the audience, in a
lowered light. Cut tattoo picture: in its place, a map of the
world, centred on the Soviet Union. Lights up, stage left, revealing a file-stacked table and three chairs, at an angle to
the screen. Seated there, a three-man TRIBUNAL: PRISIP-
KIN, ANDREYEV and SEMYONOV, smoking an even larger
cigar. Before them, stands the DIRECTOR of the mental
hospital, carrying his own file.*]

PRISIPKIN: [*Brusquely*] I presume he's still alive.

DIRECTOR: Yes.

PRISIPKIN: Pity. It would have simplified matters.

DIRECTOR: I never dreamed he'd survive.

PRISIPKIN: No need to reproach yourself.

DIRECTOR: Oh, but there is! We could have done more.

PRISIPKIN: Than what? Solitary confinement, bread and water,
no medical treatment, with a roaring fever and severe blood
poisoning?

DIRECTOR: When we turned the cameras on him a minute ago,
he was singing!

PRISIPKIN: [*Sorting his papers*] Really! What was he singing?

DIRECTOR: [*Smiling*] A children's song.

PRISIPKIN: Which one?

DIRECTOR: [*Unsuspecting*] I've no idea.

PRISIPKIN: Nonsense! Which one?

DIRECTOR: [*On his dignity*] I can't be expected—

PRISIPKIN: 'Baa baa black sheep'?

DIRECTOR: No—I—

PRISIPKIN: [*Screeching*] Which nursery rhyme was the idiot
singing?

DIRECTOR: [*Taken aback*] I'm sorry. I never thought. I....

PRISIPKIN: Comrade, you underestimate the enemy. Last week,
in Sheremestvo village, a small tea chest appeared on the Wid-
ow Shukhov's doorstep. It was labelled: 'Dung, grade one
—open when the time is ripe'. Innocent enough, you might
think. Inside, neatly folded, was the inflatable statue Shukhov
destroyed in the Hall of Heroes, plus a farrago of seditious
documents and the ice-pick which slew the traitor, Trotsky,
in his tropical hideaway.

85

SEMYONOV: [*Blowing smoke rings*] Astonishing!

PRISIPKIN: That is why every word he said, sang or muttered in his sleep should have been recorded and submitted to Intelligence for analysis.

DIRECTOR: [*Dumbfounded*] I—I didn't know.

PRISIPKIN: What kind of excuse is that? Don't you read *Truth*?

SEMYONOV: It's classified.

PRISIPKIN: What?

SEMYONOV: The Shukhov conspiracy.

PRISIPKIN: Ah! [*Suavely*] My dear fellow, do forgive me. Comrade Semyonov, you see, edits *Truth*: he is also our propaganda chief. For your, er, personal information, the Shukhov women both proved obdurate under questioning, denying all foreknowledge of the mystery dung-box.

SEMYONOV: [*More smoke*] A likely story!

PRISIPKIN: Which brings me to Shukhov himself and his latest crime. Point one: the law on tattooing of patients and prisoners is quite clear—if the offending image can be judged hostile to the State, punishment may range from gaol to execution. Point two: we have a new champion of the weightlifting world—Alexander Dobrovolsky—whose exploits [*Smiling at ANDREYEV.*] dwarfing Shukhov, have been achieved with the aid of a perfectly legal Soviet wonder compound, Lustrapods. The patient Shukhov is therefore expendable. I shall now examine the evidence in the matter. [*Calling out.*] Victor—the close-ups! [*On-screen, appears a large picture of IVAN's groin and inert penis.*] No, no, Victor, not that one! ...Really, Victor's predilection for the penis is too bad. [*The picture remains.*] Victor—cut it out!

DIRECTOR: If the tribunal will permit me to explain... [*PRISIPKIN nods.*] the penis does bear one of the tattoos. In the folds of skin you will notice—

PRISIPKIN: [*Peering at the screen*] Bigger, Victor, bigger! [*An enlargement appears.*]

DIRECTOR: There—you see! The words 'I love you'—visible on enlargement but revealed to the naked eye only when the skin is taut and the gland erect.

PRISIPKIN: Revolting!

SEMYONOV: I thought he was impotent.

ANDREYEV: [*Helplessly*] So did I.

PRISIPKIN: [*Acid*] Didn't we all? [*Shouting*] The texts, Victor, please! [*On-screen, the quotation: 'A spectre is haunting Russia—the spectre of Communism', as if written on the flesh of a man's chest.*]

DIRECTOR: [*Drily*] The quotation is taken from the prisoner's

86

right chest... [*Repeating the words.*] 'A spectre is haunting Russia—'

PRISIPKIN: [*Crossing to the screen*] I can read, can't I? I know my catechism. Look, look—upon his own flesh he perverts the prophecies of the revolution! [*On-screen, 'It is high time that Communists openly published their views'.*]

DIRECTOR: From the, er, the left breast.

PRISIPKIN: [*Exploding*] I don't believe it. The Manifesto itself abused to incite treason. [*Dramatically*] Andreyev, tell me it's not true!

ANDREYEV: It's not true, Minister.

PRISIPKIN: Certainly it's true, you buffoon—I can see it with my own eyes.

ANDREYEV: Yes, Minister. [*On-screen: 'Political power is merely the organized power of one class for oppressing another'.*]

DIRECTOR: Again, the, er, right breast, I'm afraid.

PRISIPKIN: What are you afraid of, idiot? In Russia, there are no classes. Only the State and the people. [*Screeching*] How can the State oppress the people? The State is the people! [*He bursts into a fit of coughing.*]

ANDREYEV: [*Proferring a pill*] Minister, do try to remain calm.

PRISIPKIN: [*Swallowing*] Calm? I'm perfectly calm. I am the Central Committee member for Internal Security. [*Resuming his seat, as if nothing had happened.*] Victor! [*On-screen: 'We shall have an association in which the free development of each is the condition of the free development of all'.*]

DIRECTOR: Left breast, below the nipple.

PRISIPKIN: [*Making notes in his file*] Individualism....Next! [*On-screen: 'The proletarians have nothing to lose but their chains. They have a world to win', as if written on a man's abdomen.*]

DIRECTOR: From the abdomen—near the navel.

PRISIPKIN: Where else? [*More notes.*] At last, we reach the guts of the affair. Rebellion! Yes, comrades, we face rebellion, pure and simple. [*Cut the screen quote.*]

DIRECTOR: Begging the Minister's pardon—he has seen only a fraction of the body text. All told it covers ninety five per cent of the skin area—in total, ten thousand words.

PRISIPKIN: [*Exasperated*] Summarize! [*Further relevant close-ups of IVAN's tattoos appear on-screen.*]

DIRECTOR: On the forehead, in block letters: 'I am a free man'.

PRISIPKIN: [*Not even looking up*] Most amusing.

DIRECTOR: On the torso, extracts from the Soviet legal code—

PRISIPKIN: [*Interrupting*] Covering the conduct of trials, rules of arrest, prison regulations, free speech, free assembly, free elections...we've heard it all before.

DIRECTOR: On the arms: 'I love the Union of Soviet

Socialist Republics'.

PRISIPKIN: [*Without batting an eyelid*] Is nothing sacred?

DIRECTOR: On the legs, the names of seven hundred men and women detained—

PRISIPKIN: [*Bored*] Allegedly detained.

DIRECTOR: [*Corrected*] Allegedly detained illegally in Russia.

PRISIPKIN: The list itself is illegal. Find out who compiled it.

DIRECTOR: Yes, Minister.... [*Continuing*] On both buttocks, the hammer and sickle.

PRISIPKIN: [*Triumphantly*] Ah, there we have it! Squats on the flag, does he? Thank you, Comrade Director. [*Writing in his file.*] Only one thing now perturbs me: the butterfly.

DIRECTOR: Victor—the butterfly! [*The butterfly reappears on-screen. PRISIPKIN again walks across, peering at it.*]

PRISIPKIN: I confess myself baffled by the butterfly. Intelligence require an explanation.

[*Enter, the FOURTH OFFICIAL, holding papers.*]

FOURTH OFFICIAL: May I suggest Doctor Lyubovna?

PRISIPKIN: [*Startled*] Of course!

DIRECTOR: [*Calling out*] Send for Lyubovna!

VOICES OFF: [*Echoing*] Lyubovna.... Send for Lyubovna.

PRISIPKIN: [*Consulting the file*] The woman appears to have a somewhat intimate knowledge of the case.

DIRECTOR: Most regrettable. [*Enter, VERA—calm but frightened.*]

PRISIPKIN: Ah, doctor—the prisoner Shukhov's butterfly.... Kindly elucidate.

VERA: [*Quietly*] If I refuse...?

PRISIPKIN: I would not advise it.

VERA: [*Conceding*] The butterfly is a symbol of the patient's own mortality: also of the beauty he hopes to recapture for his life: and finally, a mark of his freedom within the pattern of the corporate life we lead.

PRISIPKIN: [*Dangerously, patient*] I put it to you that the butterfly is the insignia of an anti-Soviet conspiracy.

VERA: No.

PRISIPKIN: Shukhov is a proven rebel.

VERA: How?

PRISIPKIN: On the testimony of his own flesh.

VERA: That testimony is taken exclusively from the works of Marx and Engels and our own constitution. How can it be rebellious?

PRISIPKIN: In context.

VERA: [*Bravely*] Since when, comrade, have the doctrines of Marx and Engels been subject to the theory of relativity?

PRISIPKIN: Very well, doctor: what is your judgement of

Shukhov's action?

VERA: He is mad.

PRISIPKIN: Impossible.

VERA: Why?

PRISIPKIN: Because he was mad before—in court.

VERA: So?

PRISIPKIN: He cannot be mad now.

VERA: The symptoms are constant: guilt, the search for atone-
ment, the urge to self-destruction.

PRISIPKIN: But you and I know, doctor, in the clinical sense,
Shukhov was perfectly sane at his hearing: the State simply
preferred him to be mad. If his symptoms are unchanged, he
must remain sane—in the clinical sense. And reasons of State
dictate he should be judged so. Do you quarrel, doctor, with
reasons of State?

VERA: [*Trapped*] No.

PRISIPKIN: Quite. You will now visit the prisoner to establish his
correct mental condition, in order that he may be punished
for his crimes. And remember, doctor—the tribunal will be
watching.
[*At stage left, lights down. Cut butterfly picture. Replacing
it, the Soviet flag, as at the start of the play. The sound of
clashing gates. On the darkened left-stage, the TRIBUNAL
stands, watching.... At stage right, lights up on IVAN kneeling, scratching purposefully at the floor with his knife....
VERA watches. Almost immediately, he senses her presence,
and turns to see her.*]

IVAN: [*Springing up*] Lyubovna! [*Pause. They look at each
other.*]

VERA: What are you doing?

IVAN: [*With a grin*] Escapin'.

VERA: Don't be ridiculous. [*She glances anxiously towards the
TRIBUNAL.*]

IVAN: I'm going to dig my way out.

VERA: What with?

IVAN: Knife and fork. [*Showing them to her.*] It's a piece of
cake. I mean it.

VERA: [*Smiling*] Do you know how thick that wall is?

IVAN: [*Casually*] Ten foot.

VERA: You haven't a chance. It'd take months.

IVAN: Good. That'll leave plenty time to write my book.

VERA: Shukhov! Stop it!

IVAN: [*Blithely*] Didn't I tell you about my book? I'll beg for
Comrade Stalin's collected works, then write between the
lines.

VERA: Stop it!

IVAN: I'm going to tell the truth—like Gavrilov...only I'll tell it in blood...I'm sick of ink.

VERA: Stop it! [*Calming*] I'm not here to play games.

IVAN: No, doctor, you've come to interview me for the hospital television service.... Where's the camera, doctor? Over here? Over here? Yeah, over here. [*He faces the TRIBUNAL, across the stage.*] Got the picture, comrades? What's the punishment these days for telling the truth? Do you rip out my tongue? An' if I write it down, do you chop off my hands? An' if I learn to write with my toes, do you cut off my feet? An' if I write with my mouth, do you pull out my teeth—or chop off my head? Is that it, comrades? Off with his head! Stop me writing, wouldn't it? Wouldn't stop the blood, though—heart's blood, comrades, spilling out under the cell door an' down the iron steps an' along the corridors an' across the courtyard an' through the gates an' into the streets, until people saw it on their boots, comrades, an' started to ask: 'What the devil's going on in the loony bin?' Not that it matters much, does it? Here comes the director an' ses to his doctors: 'Why is this heart still beating? Remove it at once—an' mop up the mess!' Ah, but could they lift it, though, comrades—heart like mine? It'd drop through their hands! It'd drop through the world! I tell you, it'd shoot from the sea in a shower of sparks, pumping blood into the sky, turnin' the sun crimson, pouring a red rain on the earth —great drops o' blood, comrades, that drip at night, endlessly, drip, drip, on the sleepless foreheads of your torturers an' your men of power, till they cry out with pain an' confess they've betrayed the revolution! An' these same traitors, comrades, they'll be condemned to seek out that failing heart, Mother Russia's heart, an' catch it where it falls, bled near to white, but beating still, an' bring it safe to Sheremestvo, south of Krasnodar, an' set it free there in the cornfields, full o' red flowers. [*Turning, in his exultation, he sees VERA, leaning against the wall in despair. He rushes to her.*] Doctor, the heart, the butterfly heart—it'd flutter down into the old mine at Sheremestvo, [*Slowly VERA turns to him.*] it'd settle on a broken body, lying like crystal, in the low seam, and at the beating of its wings in the great hole where it once belonged, that corpse would stir, in the darkness of the mine at Sheremestvo, and the New Man would walk out, hidden in the crowd of the evening shift, carrying his lamp an' snap tin, labelled 'Ivan Shukhov', limping home to his wife and his patient mother, rejoicing at the stars in the night sky, the silver seeds of another day's threshing.... [*He seizes VERA's hands, willing her to feel his elation.*] Say you believe me!

VERA: [*After pause*] I believe you....

IVAN: One day, the revolution'll set us free, among the people
—all of us, free, together.... [*VERA weeps.*] Don't cry....
I'm happy. I'm making a start.

VERA: They'll be coming for you soon.

IVAN: [*Smiling*] I know.... And you?

VERA: Yes.... Goodbye.

IVAN: Goodbye.... Remember me.

VERA: Always. [*She exits—without a glance back. Straight away,
IVAN renews his scratching. The lights, stage right, dim a little.
Lights up, stage left. The TRIBUNAL is in final session.*]

ANDREYEV: He really is mad.

PRISIPKIN: Ironic, isn't it? Director, see that Lyubovna signs
Shukhov's hospital release. She is then to be discharged with
dishonour and moved to auxiliary nursing duties in the snow-
country.

DIRECTOR: Yes, Minister, at once, Minister. [*He exits.*]

PRISIPKIN: Now, comrades, how do we find on Shukhov?

SEMYONOV: Guilty.

PRISIPKIN: On all counts?

ANDREYEV: On all counts. [*The FOURTH OFFICIAL hands
PRISIPKIN a paper, which he absorbs at a glance.*]

PRISIPKIN: Excellent. We could execute him: we could flay the
skin from his dreadful body. But we are not savages, comrades
—unlike the prisoner, who paints his flesh as a pygmy, where
once he was a flawless giant. Comrades, Shukhov shall live
—but no one shall see him live: no one shall see what he has
made of himself. The sentence is: solitary confinement until
death. Agreed?

SEMYONOV: Agreed.

ANDREYEV: Agreed.

PRISIPKIN: [*Standing*] The conspiracy shall be crushed. The
butterfly will die in the darkness: tomorrow, the new day
shall dawn! [*Lights down, stage left. Cut screen-picture. At
stage right, IVAN, spotlit now, on his knees, resumes his song
confidently, clearly.*]

IVAN: [*Singing*]
> But if you would sing with me,
> you'll not need a cent, you see:
> so, come and sing together—
> if you dance then you will need
> boots of shining leather....

[*With his knife, he scratches away at the stage floor. The lights
dim. He works on. Eventually, the whole stage is blacked out.
Still the scratching is heard in the darkness—growing now,
until it fills the auditorium.*]